Black Velvet

on

White Satin

A HISTORIC ROMANCE NOVEL SET IN THE TURBULENT 60S

JEANNIE PIAZZA

Published by Hemingway Publishers

Cover design by Hemingway Publishers

ISBN: Printed in the United States

Author Jeannie Piazza

"The Work Began In May, 2021"

ABOUT THE AUTHOR

Jeannie Piazza-Zuniga is the author of *The Magic of the Olympia Theater, A Peek Behind Its Curtain, Drama On and Off Stage at Gusman Center*, a memoir of her career from Florida International University student-intern to Director of Theater Operations in the City of Miami's historic treasure, the Olympia Theater. A story of how the decaying Theater came to life and filled the downtown with new excitement through the '70s into 2001.The magnificent historic Olympia Theater has fallen into decay as it celebrates its 100th Birthday.

Her second book is a novel about two people whose love for the law brings them together in the '60s in New England in an unlawful love. She is white, and he is Black. A combination most disagreeable to many, as bigotry was at a high pitch and promised to get worse. Jen is a child of means with a stern father who manages to steer her in the direction he has chosen for her life. How will she handle his bigotry and the love of this extraordinary Black man?

Ms. Piazza-Zuniga, in her senior year of high school, was crowned Miss Medford, after which she went on to study at the New England Conservatory of Music. She graduated from Burdett College of Business and Florida International University's Theater Department. She taught for Miami-Dade Public Schools for over 25 years and continues to be involved with the arts, music, and writing. She has been published in the *Miami Herald, Preservation Magazine* and more.

DEDICATION

This book is dedicated in Memory of

Auntie Jennie Piazza

TABLE OF CONTENTS

PRESENT

Massachusetts, October 1965

It is night in the cool countryside outside Boston. Jen sat alone in the living room, watching the rainstorm swirl the autumn leaves into mesmerizing shapes. The wind sculptured the blowing colors into eerie, ghostly streams as Jen listened to the mellow, aching tones of Nina Simone. Her skin tingles with the warmth generated by the dancing flames in the fireplace. She feels, as she had always felt at moments like this, excited anticipation—that inexplicable sense that something is about to begin, a new chapter or the end of something. But for certain, a serious decision must be made.

Was her life heading toward a future of unparalleled happiness or unbearable heartbreaks? Her father had warned her often: the world is relentlessly unforgiving, a tough and ruthless environment. He felt she was not ready to push back against the bigotry of the courts or to defy their dismissive attitude toward women on the bench. He sensed that the power of the law and the greed of politics would crush her kind soul.

What Dad didn't know was that Jen knew and understood all that he said. She knew that, in the '60s, being a female attorney was an uphill battle. Women with law degrees are still being pushed toward secretarial roles instead of courtrooms. But she must set all that aside—for now.

Because Jen faces an even greater challenge. She is falling in love with a brilliant, charismatic attorney. Handsome, successful, and driven, he has his sights on a campaign for Governor. And, he wants her—desperately. Wants her love, her partnership, a life together with a family.

The only problem is her parents, though loving and controlling… are bigots. They had unexpectedly found out that the man she loves, the man who may shape her future, is Black. What is her future? How will she find the balance?

CHAPTER 1

(Flashback)

Winter–Massachusetts, December 1964

The destructive riots had begun. Over 329 riots wreaked havoc through 257 cities in the U.S., from as far south as Miami, extending to riots rising from the Deep South upward into the north in the poverty-stricken areas of Roxbury, straight through Dorchester Avenue in Boston. It was the late '60s. Yet the stability of life continued in the State House of Boston, Massachusetts.

The golden dome of the State House glimmered under the dazzling winter sun. It shimmered with exuberance generated by the enthusiasm under the dome in the offices of the Attorney General. The staff had just learned that Massachusetts and the Attorney General would host the National Conference of Attorneys General in the spring of 1965. As such, our Attorney General directed all departments to "straighten up" their areas for the influx of visitors to our offices from other states.

"We want to show our efficiency and organization in every possible way, even though most meetings will take place at the Hilton Hotel across the Common from the State House," he proudly announced.

The Attorney General described the conference procedures that would be followed and the subjects that might be addressed throughout the week, but that further information would follow as more details were decided.

In a later meeting, he asked the staff to establish a journal in each department so that the Assistant Attorneys General and administrative secretarial personnel could sign up for the legal and secretarial duties required in the committee rooms to be set up at the hotel for the week.

For all those who signed up to work in the secretarial pool, each would provide that information to the Task Force Team, or what some staffers called "the Angels of Doom," dedicated to protecting the Boss from everyone. Several committees would be formed, each covering serious national issues of the law, such as desegregation, an issue that was beginning to create major dissent across the country. The country's most pressing dilemmas: desegregation, urban unrest, and the crippling cost of fuel in northern winters would be discussed in committee by legal minds. The results would be recorded in draft by secretarial staff, debates transcribed, and policies shaped into print to produce a book for each attorney general to take home to his constituents.

During that week in our city, the body of legal minds would discuss issues especially pertinent to their state, as well as those suffered by our state. The dilemma for most northern states, almost every winter, was the several months of extremely low temperatures and higher-than-usual fuel rates. Additional fuel was always desperately needed in our area during winter. Solutions would be suggested, and the writings on the issue would be drafted by administrative assistants and ultimately compiled into a book for presentation on the final days of the conference to each Attorney General. We also faced the issues of integration, its effects upon the school system, and the rioting taking place in the Boston area. Further instructions would be forthcoming as the time drew near. Although the many issues were deeply serious, there would be many fun cocktail gatherings and formal dinner parties, too, for the visiting Attorneys General.

All this indicated that staff would utilize their outstanding skills—those with which they had acquired their positions in this office in the first place. They would now apply those skills in the performance of a week of tasks under unbelievably arduous conditions.

Later in the year, at the next meeting of the Conference, our Boss stated, "To achieve quality for a successful conference, each department will be assigned a task force of a number of assistant AGs for legal guidance and administrative secretaries to take notes, type the discussions, and assist members of the committees with whatever might be required."

The idea of a week of intense, concentrated legal work excited Jen, a soon-to-be graduate law student, lucky enough to have a position in the Department of the Attorney General. She was stimulated by the challenges of the various legal subjects to be covered, and the hotly debated issues on desegregation, which were in many of the briefs Jen typed, further stimulated her interest. The boss told staff there would be no additional hourly pay and that, more than likely, volunteer staff would work longer hours, with an earlier starting time and later than the 5 p.m. finish. Any overtime would be given as accrued time off. Motivated and eager, Jen got to her department. She set up the sheet for sign-in and immediately signed up. The extra hours were of no consequence to her. Jen lived alone in a lovely house in the country, had no husband or children to worry about, and was lucky enough to have a small, sparsely furnished studio apartment down the street from her job in the State House.

"Neither sleet, nor snow, nor torrents of rain could keep me from a day's work," she laughingly told her bosses. Jen loved the work and the direction of her life. A special joy filled her heart daily the moment she walked into the incredible State House. The building itself held a sense of power that flowed through everyone upon initial entry. Walking through the Hall of Flags uplifted a sense of soldiering that further gave a sense of pride and honor for those men and women who fought for freedom. Just being there, Jen felt a patriotic honor.

Jen felt that the administrative work she performed for the Department of the Attorney General gave her a sense of pride, too. With high expenses, a second job at cousin Nick's auto rental, a few blocks away, was helpful. It allowed Jen to keep the little studio apartment a block from the State House and to pay for the extra amenities she treasured. Now, the sweetest attraction of working overtime hours without pay on this project was not the work itself but rather the party invitations for many of the secretaries. If we worked on a committee, we would be allowed to attend one party with a day of our choice off with pay. The "Angels of Doom" would review and send out the one invitation to those who qualified. It all worked out perfectly. JR, as his personal staff referred to him, was the second attorney general for whom Jen worked. JR admired her work and kept Jen on his staff, though she was not a civil servant. Jen tested higher than any support staff who took the test, and she was dedicated to her work. She was also charming and fun to be around, aside from being quite beautiful. JR noticed Jen. Jen felt very blessed. Those who labored as volunteers on campaigns got some jobs. Jen was neither. However, she did vote for him. Each day, new objectives had to be achieved to hold this position.

Jen loved being in the State House. She often walked through the Hall of Flags to peek into the House of Representatives. Whether the House was in session or not, the magnificence of the Hall charged her spirit. As a result, the party invitation really slipped her mind. Also, the girls in the front office seemed to tolerate her but not befriend her. Jen had little time to develop close friends in the department and hardly anyone to go to parties with. So, she put all that aside and focused on the tasks ahead.

The winter months passed, leaving the citizens of the city with high-priced oil heating bills as well as hefty bills for the removal of mountains of ice and snowdrifts needing to be plowed to avoid obstructing clear views for drivers. However, if we wait a bit, the winter sun will come shining through to melt the snow and make a path for Spring. The crocuses will peek their flowering colors out from under the warming ground, and the trees will begin to burst forth their leaves from the heat of the strengthening sun. Spring will arrive, and the 1965 Conference of State Attorneys General will be at our door.

On the Friday before the first day of the Conference and the arrival of the nation's top legal minds, Jen prepared a box of essential secretarial items: paper, pens, carbon sheets, dictation pads, and pencils. She felt she needed these to set up her desk at the hotel. Jen always prepared for her needs while not relying on others for them. Nancy, the young but motherly receptionist in the Executive Department, who lived vicariously through many of Jen's activities and stories, picked up the ringing phone, answered it, then covered the mouthpiece, saying, "It's the boss's right hand, and she wants to talk to you."

Jen took the call, shrugging her shoulders with a look indicating, "I wonder what it's about?"

"Hello."

"Hello. Hi, Jen, is everything ready? All is okay?"

"Yes, of course."

"Are you ready for Monday? Is there anything that you need?"

Jen wondered why she was calling her, but she answered. "Yes. No, I have everything I need, and I will be at the Hilton Hotel early on Monday. I expect to be there at 7:30 AM."

"That's great, but JR wants to know why we don't have your RSVP invitation response? Did you forget?"

"Well… yes… uh, but… no, it seems I never got my invitation."

"Oh, wait one minute." She spoke to the boss in a conversation I could not hear. Returning to our conversation, she said, "JR wants to know if it is not too late for you to arrange it; you might consider coming to one, or all, the parties—whichever ones you are able to attend?"

"Oh my gosh, I can't believe this!" went off in Jen's head. She was speechless. She had forgotten about that one party most everyone wanted to attend, not for the grueling workload attached. She was jumping out of her skin with joy.

"I'll go to ALL of them!" Jen joyfully thought.

"Uh, no… uh, yes… I mean, uh, thank you so much. I will be there. Thank you."

Why hadn't Jen received the invitation? That's an easy one. The invitation must have gotten lost in transit. The Angels of Doom were in charge of the invitations. They watched over JR as if he were one step away from sainthood. They protected him from anyone they thought might request something from him, especially an attractive female.

This group hardly spoke to Jen, even at office gatherings. No matter. Jen's interest was to do the best work possible to continue working in the department, and to go to law school at Suffolk University, conveniently located behind the State House. Other nights, she was the front desk star at cousin Nick's auto rental down the street from the State House. Nick always said, "You're a real looker, Jen, and the customers love you." So, her life was hectic, stimulating, and family-centered.

CHAPTER 2

Monday came with the sunrise. A lovely April spring day was its reward. Jen arrived early at the hotel to set up her area, preparing for the day's work. She was early and the only one there other than the hotel staff. Once the conference began, there were strenuous and demanding days ahead. Jen paced herself.

She got through Monday and Tuesday, not going to any of the parties. However, by Wednesday, the BBQ Lunch Cruise around Boston Harbor to Fort Independence on Castle Island charged her enthusiasm. It was a historic cruise with tales of the Revolutionary War in 1775, when the American colonies wished to secede from England. The Lunch Cruise promised to be great fun as everyone would be more relaxed than at any of the next events, which were of a more formal tone. The cruise truly was a fun party. Apparently, everyone wanted to be on this cruise. They packed the cruise boat to its legal capacity. Everyone had a joke or two to tell, just as Jen did. Due to her strict upbringing, Jen was a little hesitant to be so outspoken. She had a shy side to her personality, which she constantly fought. Actually, it was fear implanted in her by her always-frightened mother. With a bit of encouragement from some of the Assistant Attorneys General, Jen decided she would tell her cute but naughty story. There was a Deputy AG in the office who had recently become divorced and was dating a lady that the gossipy staff felt was not up to his stature, yet he was head over heels for her. When this woman came into the office, looking like a Marilyn Monroe cutout but not as pretty, he became "unglued." Knowing all that, Jen thought she had the perfect story to tell the partying cluster of staff and visitors around her, while never mentioning anyone specific. It was safe to tell the story since few had knowledge of who, if anyone, it was really about.

"This is a story about a little mouse," Jen began as the crowd became silenced.

"A little mouse was out for a walk, whistling as he danced along the railroad tracks on a lovely, warm summer day, feeling so happy and pleased with himself. He looked up at the beautiful blue sky, whistled at the white clouds, and paid no attention to anything as he twirled and hopped playfully on the tracks. Suddenly, at that moment, a train came speeding through and WACK!—sliced off a piece of his tail. He was so upset. He bounced around again, not noticing the other train coming in the opposite direction. As it sped by, ZAP!—it sliced off the little mouse's head. The moral of the story is 'Never lose your head over a piece of tail.'"

The story was a success, judging by thunderous applause and cheers. Some of the staff who never acknowledged Jen gave her a thumbs-up or a pat on the back. However, she had to be careful not to lose HER head. The party Jen really wanted to attend was the Thursday night Greet & Meet Cocktail Party at the Hotel in the Main Ballroom. She now had an invitation to it.

She had packed a sleek black dress that displayed the sensuous curves of her voluptuous body, with a cinched waistband that enhanced her small waistline just above curved hips, flowing down to slim, strong legs paired with size five black pumps, and a sparkly shawl for an elegant flair to keep her comfortable in the cool ballroom. Jen left the hotel after a busy day and walked to her studio, 15 minutes away, to shower and dress for the evening. After all the preparations, Jen was ready. She took a cab from the studio apartment back to the hotel to avoid being disheveled by a walk across the Common in high heels and a cool spring wind that might tousle her hair.

Jen entered the hotel and walked through the elegantly designed lobby of mirrors, remembering the feeling she had while visiting the Palace of Versailles on a family vacation. Now, she experienced the elegance of the exquisitely lit crystal chandeliers of the hotel, as though she were in the Hall of Mirrors in the Palace of Versailles. Jen walked through the reflective hall leading to the room where the Attorneys General Conference Cocktail Party was in full swing. At the hotel that night, Jen felt sensually elegant as she confidently passed the many distinguished men clustered in conversational groups. Then she passed the Angels of Doom, who seldom, if ever, acknowledged her. But tonight, though a little nervous being alone, she felt good—confident in the choice of the black sheath, with her blond hair in a fashionably fetching French twist—a perfect fit for any palace.

She was certain the Angels of Doom wondered, *"How did she get here?"* For their part, Jen would never have received an invitation if the boss hadn't noticed the slight and called to invite Jen personally.

As Jen entered the ballroom, she glanced over the room, seeking a friendly face to return her smile and allow her to approach their conversation. It worked. She walked over to the Assistant Attorney General of the Consumer Protection Division, with whom she had a good relationship. They spoke for a moment. Then Jen excused herself to walk across the ballroom to the bar for the one drink of the night—a Dewar's on the rocks. After getting her Dewar's, she turned to walk back across the floor, but as she did, a very handsome, bronzed-skin man with distinguishing sculptured features, closely cropped curly black hair, and an outrageously strong, toned body—looking younger than the boss—stopped her in her path. It was clever the way he managed to corner Jen in a space without corners. He was gorgeous, with eyes of blue-green and a twinkle that darted straight to her heart. Yet Jen's heart set up a safety net that silently shouted *STOP* when trouble was ahead. In the soft lighting of the room, Jen could not distinguish his blackness. His smile displayed a perfect set of white teeth that sparkled when he smiled. She had to gather every bit of protocol to keep from displaying her restless sensuality.

"Hi, I'm Brason."

"Well, hello, Brason. I'm Jen."

"I've seen you in the committee meetings and especially enjoyed your moral's story on the lunch cruise. I agree that no one should lose his or her head over a piece of tail."

Jen laughed, slightly embarrassed. "Are you enjoying the work being done in committee?"

"Oh yes. I am having a wonderful time working with the committee members. Would you like to sit at that table?" He pointed to an empty table for two.

They sat at the nearby table, possibly creating immediate office chatter. What the week was turning into was everyone's guess. Before too long, others of his party gathered around, creating a party within a party.

"I am so happy I came alone to this one," she silently applauded her decision. *"If this were the only party I came to, I should consider it a jackpot selection,"* she concluded.

It was an incredibly fun and intellectually stimulating evening so far. Brason was not only strikingly handsome but also loquacious and charming. However, his joyful group was going to party on to another restaurant to continue their evening with a delicious steak at Teresa's.

Brason asked Jen to go along with them. But as much as she wanted to go, she knew tomorrow was a busy and final day of committee meetings. It was time to complete the books for the printer so as to be ready for the Attorney General to take a copy home. Almost everyone would be leaving on Saturday morning, so there was a lot of work to finish. Jen thanked Brason and gave him her honest reason for not joining them.

"After all, I am here to work, not party. My work always comes before my partying." He was very kind in his acceptance of the reason for not going. However, he also appeared disappointed at having to wait until tomorrow to see her again.

He said, "See you tomorrow?" as they walked through the lobby to the front of the hotel, where the valet waited to fetch their automobiles or taxis.

"Yes, I will get a cab back to my apartment." Jen waved a sad au revoir to her newfound handsome Attorney General. Standing very close by was Scott, the security police officer who was always around when the boss was anywhere. He had walked beside them as they walked through the hotel.

"I'll take you home." It was Scott. He must have been part of Brason's security cover, or must have at least been released from duty to offer this convenience. Jen was happy to accept the company home, because the Common and Gardens were not exactly safe for a young woman walking alone at night. This guy, Scott, was an outlandishly handsome young man. All the girls in the State House wanted to date him, but he seemed not to pay much attention to anyone. Of course, he was almost always on duty. Anyone could only imagine what the Angels of Doom thought when they saw Jen leave the ballroom with both the handsome, amazingly shaped security escort, while waving goodbye to the handsome Attorney General Jen had spent the past several hours with. Scott gave the valet his ticket, and they waited for the delivery of his automobile as the rest of the party got into several cars going to their next destination. Jen really wanted to go, but knew it best on many levels that she did not.

CHAPTER 3

Jen's security escort was very talkative as she gave him the address to the studio. It was a very short drive, and fortunately, there was a parking spot at the building. Jen thanked him for a safe delivery without asking him up; however, he got out of the car, came around to open the passenger-side door, and helped her out.

"You are safe only when I have left you in your apartment."

"Okay, it sounds like a plan, but I must assure you that although the address is Beacon Hill, you will see that my decorator quit quite early in the project."

Both laughed as they climbed the stairs to the third floor. On the first floor, there was a drugstore-pharmacy, and no elevator to any of the five floors.

"Well, you've come this far—you might as well come in for a moment. I can offer you a cup of water, a glass of water, or a bottle of water, if you like. What will you have?"

"Yes, I guess maybe… I would like… I'll take a glass of water," he said, and they both chuckled.

"I agree, your decorator must have left you in a big hurry," he said, as he perused the surroundings.

"Yes, but do notice the one thing my studio does have: old but interesting real hardwood floors, blotched with an artist's paint droppings to verify the story of its past artists' occupancy. The sofa bed, which I invite you to sit on while I get you your exotic drink, was left behind by possibly several tenants before me. I love how it is centered before the three large bay windows with no curtains, looking out onto Charles Street, one of Boston's most charming old Beacon Hill neighborhoods, with gaslight lampposts on each street corner.

"Well, this is my little hideaway that allows me to get through the winters without suffering the daily 50-mile drive to work and the 50-mile drive back home at the end of a tiring day, regardless of the weather. And as far as dating, the comments around town are that I am 'geographically undesirable' and just too much trouble to date. But that's okay with me because I don't have much time for dating."

They continued talking.

"You, too much trouble to date?"

"Yes, it was big trouble for anyone to come to where I live. I live in the country just outside the New Hampshire line. Most of the time, if I had a date, I would meet them in Boston or at their apartment, leave my car in their garage, go to dinner, pick up my car, say goodnight, and drive home. I didn't drink much more than maybe one or two drinks in an entire evening, so I was always prepared to drive home or stay at the studio.

"I heard something about you. Would you verify it for me?"

"Certainly, if I can."

"Is it true that you pick up our Attorney General every morning at 6 AM, and you drive to a nearby beach to run in the sand for an hour, rain or shine? Then it is direct to the gym for other exercise, showers, dressing, and off to the State House for the day's work?"

"Aha!" he said while nodding.

"WOW!"

Scott told Jen that night that he would accompany the Attorney General to any political functions he might have to attend. Scott was at the boss's beck and call. He loved his work. He respected and admired JR. He was proud of the honor that JR had selected him as his personal security.

As their animated conversation continued, Scott received a call on his connector—or walkie-talkie, or whatever he was using. Jen had no phone in her studio, and there were no personal phones at this time for the everyday staff. She heard him answer "yes" to whoever was making the call. Then, after a few more "yeses," he handed the instrument over to her, saying, "He wants to speak to you."

"He? Who's he?"

Jen couldn't imagine who would be calling her on his phone, but she answered with firmness. "Hello. Yes, this is Jen."

"Please wait," an unfamiliar voice instructed.

"Hi, Jen, this is Brason. I couldn't wait until tomorrow. How are you doing?"

"I'm doing fine, but it sounds as if you are having a grand ol' time."

"Yes, everyone is being absolutely gracious hosts to me. I just wanted to hear that you got home safely."

"Yes, Scott has brought me home safe and sound. We are coming to the end of our conversation, and soon he will leave."

"Before I say goodnight, Jen, I wonder, only if you are free and might want to, would you be my dinner partner for the Friday night formal party at The Wharf tomorrow evening?"

"I can't think of a better way to end this extraordinary conference. Yes, I would love to be your dinner partner tomorrow."

"Now, I can sleep peacefully tonight, happy knowing I will see you tomorrow and be with you for dinner tomorrow night."

"Me too. Be careful getting back to the hotel, and sleep well, Brason."

With that, Jen handed over the phone to Scott, who stood up to indicate that the conversations had ended—and that he knew enough about Jen to report to JR, or even Brason, if that had been part of the decision to drive her home. No one would ever know.

"Thank you so much, Scott. You are a dear to take the time to see me home. I will certainly see you tomorrow."

"Sleep well, little girl. You have a busy day tomorrow," Scott said as he started down the three stories he had climbed.

"Yes, I will, and thanks again." Jen closed the door and headed for the sofa bed, ready for a night of anticipatory dreams and absorption of the day's thrilling experiences. The dreams of tonight would surely bring unexpected treasures of memories tomorrow.

Sleep did not come easily, even though Jen was really exhausted from the week's workload. But when she finally slept, it was with visions of all the hopes any single young woman dreams of. She slept happily and deeply.

As the sun rose, it cast sunlight streaming through the three uncovered bay windows, causing streaks of colored light to fill the room. Jen woke, fully understanding the reason it was an artist's studio—the light. The sheer fullness of the light made Jen want to paint, though that was not one of her best qualities. Instead, she danced barefoot on this fabulous wood floor and exercised to prepare for the exhilarating, unknowing kind of day it would bring. Jen loved this type of day. Anything could happen. She glowed in its covert possibilities as she danced around.

Jen showered, then packed the travel cosmetic bag and a change of clothes for the next day. She placed the long cream-colored formal dress in its carrier bag. She loved this gown, with its off-the-shoulder beaded ruffle that lay softly over a deep V neckline. It was one of the prettiest gowns in her closet—not sexy or revealing, just girlishly soft, flowing into a lovely A-line. There were others in her closet, but this showed the elegance, beauty, and charm of a girl growing into womanhood. Even though Jen had a voluptuous figure, she tried to conceal it. She was really uncomfortable with sex. It resulted from a strict Catholic upbringing and her father holding on to old-school values. Despite the freedom of the '60s, Jen was still quite shy about the freedom it brought.

Her only thought for the moment was to get her car out of the State House parking spot and place all the items she would need for the day, plus the gown and shoes for the evening formal dinner. She must not forget the Saturday morning change for the return home to the country. The plan was to bring the car to the hotel parking garage so that all the required clothes were in the car. She could get dressed in the Hospitality Suite assigned to the conference before going to the cocktail party and dinner with Brason. She would return to the hotel after dinner, pick up her car to either get home to the country or back to the studio after the entire day's activities. That was her plan.

CHAPTER 4

Jen got to the hotel early for the coffee shop's perfect breakfast of egg, toast, and tea. Brason was sitting there with other Attorneys General. He motioned her to join them. Everyone was satisfied with the events of the week. And now, the final, most enchanting evening of them all was ahead. The day began with a barrage of committee members gathering all the work and equipment they had used during the week. Notes that had been placed in folders for them to take back to their states, and mementos of their stay in Boston, were gathered. How anyone had time to see Boston beyond what the parties showed was a stretch of the imagination. Brason held Jen back as the crowd dispersed for their committee.

"Look, Jen, I have a cocktail party in one of the suites with a few attorneys from some states in which I have a particular interest. I would invite you, but it is business. I will be dressed in a tuxedo early and ready to go to the party. If you do not have a place to get ready, you may use my room. I will call you from the front desk when I am finished with the short meeting, and you can come to meet me. Cocktails at The Wharf begin at 6:30 p.m., so let's say we meet at 6:00 p.m. in the Lobby by the sculpture. The limousine will pick us up at the front door of the hotel."

"Perfect. I've brought my clothes, and I'm leaving my car in the hotel garage. I am so excited. Remind me to tell you later why I am so excited."

"Okay, have a nice day, Jen. I am looking forward to being with you this evening."

"I am too. It will be fun." They left each other to finish the final committee meetings of the Conference. Both anticipated a fabulous evening ahead.

"It might be over on Saturday, but we still have tonight," went through Jen's mind.

It took every bit of concentration for Jen to keep her mind on finishing the committee's work. Her mind kept envisioning the events of the evening. In an attempt not to be disappointed, she often preferred to just let life happen. They had very little time to get to know each other, except in the committee room. There was so much to learn about one another. Would it be possible to learn all the pertinent information during dinner, with all the other Attorneys General at their table, talking about the wonder of our gloriously historic city, while the orchestra would, more than likely, play inviting dance music? Jen tried not to watch the clock in the committee room, allowing for it to move quickly, but each tick was hours long; so it seemed.

At last, it was time for Jen to close the last box and mark it for pickup by the crew who would deliver it to the State House. Brason had given Jen the key to his suite, which she tucked safely into the pocket of her suit jacket. She touched it to assure herself that it was real, and this was what she was to do: go to his suite, shower, reapply makeup, style her hair in a sweeping updo with some added curls, and dress in the most elegant gown. All that would take about an hour and a half. The clock showed 4:00, giving her just enough time to complete the transformation and join Brason in the lobby. Jen left the committee room and headed for the elevators. She stepped into a fully packed elevator, pressed the button to the floor, and enjoyed the ride up to her floor—not "her floor" but rather Brason's floor. Excitement raced through her stomach, though her nerves remained calm. She was certain that tonight would be a special moment, whether one dinner date or something more; no matter what happened, it would be remembered in her heart all her life. As the floor number showed, she excused herself from the crushing elevator crowd just as a voice from the back corner shouted, "Jen, will we see you tonight?"

"I hope so," she replied to an Attorney General from Georgia in the back row as she stepped out of the elevator.

There was no one in the corridor. Jen looked to find the door number to match the number on the key. Never good with keys, this one gave her no difficulty. Maybe that was a good sign; all would be good tonight. The door opened into a suite you might see in a movie. As one entered, a foyer with a round table in the center held a large bouquet of spring flowers in a sparkling crystal vase. The soft, welcoming, indirect lights emitted a cozy feeling in the fireplace living room. The blue, white, and navy-colored sofas and side chairs formed a perfect conversational grouping.

"I wonder if Brason's cocktail meeting is in another suite just as elegantly decorated?" Jen questioned the empty room. She placed the luggage, carried from the car, on the bench at the foot of the bed. The decoration in this room enhanced the colors of the living room with a headboard of tufting that matched the bed covering. Overhead lighting was enhanced by Tiffany-shaded lamps on either side of the king-size bed. The bathroom was a combination of toilet and bidet in its own cubicle with a closed door, a double-sink vanity of blue marble with a full wall of lighted mirrors, and then a shower large enough for two, of white marble grained with a slight hint of blue streaks.

"I must be in a dream," she thought as she pinched herself. *"Ouch, that hurt."* She was talking to herself again, but was quite

excited to hurry. She had to be showered, ready and out the door by 5:55 p.m. to meet Brason at 6:00. She was excited but surprisingly calm and eager to be the dinner partner of this charming, intelligent, handsome man.

"Oh, if they could only see me now, those catty office gals. Like in the musical Sweet Charity goes: All I can say is 'WOW... look at where I'm at, they'd never believe me... if my friends could see me... if my friends could see me now!' Well, those Angels of Doom will certainly see me as I exit the limousine and walk into the formal cocktail party on the arm of Attorney General Brason Washington."

Jen finished hairstyling with extra volume supplied by a curly hairpiece that added more dimension yet softness to the look, followed by makeup. With both perfect, she was ready for the gown. She carefully took it out of the carrier, slid it over her head without touching her hair or makeup, then slipped on the beige Cinderella dance shoes, ready to do some dancing. She added a gold hand purse and placed a white linen handkerchief in its pocket. She was ready… ready for whatever tonight held. She might not have been here tonight. But somehow, her Fairy Godmother must have been hiding in the weeds. Jen took a deep breath and twirled 360 degrees to see the circular flow of the gown. It was all quite perfect.

"Please, God, help me through this evening; let it be wonderful."

Jen tidied up the bathroom, folded the towels she had used on the bench in the shower, and ran a face cloth over the vanity, clearing away all the watermarks. She wanted it to appear as if no one had been here. She left her overnight case in the corner, not wanting to open his closet with a last look. Everything was ready.

"Okay, world, here I come," she said as she picked up the key, placed it in her purse, and closed the door behind her.

CHAPTER 5

On the ride down in the elevator, Jen felt as if she were entering a grand entrance into another world, like the fairy tales she loved so much to watch. There was a direct visual line to the sculpture where Brason should have been standing. She did not see him; her heart skipped a beat. "What if he's not here?" Butterflies fluttered in her stomach, but she walked with stately purpose. Then, just behind the sculpture where the phones to the rooms were located, she saw him put down the phone as they caught each other's eye. Brason stood there with an expression that showed he liked what he saw. He watched as Jen floated toward him. He walked toward her quickly, shortening the distance between them. When he reached her, he took her hand and kissed it. Then, as he moved close to her face, he kissed one cheek, then the other, and whispered in her ear, "You are astonishingly beautiful, Jen. Tonight will be wonderful." He took his place beside her. Jen nestled her arm through his as they walked through the lobby to the waiting limousine for the ride to the Wharf, while onlookers watched this stunning mixed-race couple walk to the limo.

On the ride to dinner, Brason continued to compliment Jen on how lovely she looked. However, he was also articulate about her administrative performance over the past week in committee, which especially pleased Jen.

"You're blushing," he cajoled, just as the limousine drove down Charles Street toward Storrow Drive, passing the Boston Common on the right.

To take the conversation away from what triggered the blush, Jen began spouting facts about the Common.

"To your right, sir, is America's oldest public park, dating back to 1634."

"You don't say?" he teased.

"Yes, I do say. Governor John Winthrop, an English Puritan lawyer and founder of the Massachusetts Bay Colony, established the second major settlement in New England."

"Okay, but can you tell me what was the first?"

"The first was, of course, where the Pilgrims are said to have landed—the Plymouth Colony. And do you know that the Pilgrims left from the steps of their small town called Plymouth and landed in the New World on land they called Plymouth? Not much imagination, I'd say."

Continuing almost on the same breath, "Also, Governor Winthrop, who they called *the American Moses* because he led his followers for 12 years beginning in 1630, pitched tents on the 48 acres of the land of the Common while he lived on the upper slope of Beacon Hill overlooking an expansion of meadow that ran down the western side of Back Bay. Also, there was a Rev. Blackstone who owned the crest of the hill. He kept a piece and then sold the remaining meadow to the town in 1634. The Puritans, accustomed to 'common land,' reserved the land for common use, and that's the Boston Common."

Brason watched Jen as she excitedly sounded like a professional tourist guide for the Massachusetts Visitors Bureau. Before she could take another breath to continue, he took her hand and kissed it again, which stopped her commentary.

"Are you nervous?" Brason asked in a gentle, non-accusing voice.

"I'm rattling on, huh?"

"Well, maybe just a tiny bit."

"I get so excited about my city, its history. And maybe I'm a tiny bit nervous."

"Don't be. You look beautiful, you are smart, and I am proud you agreed to be my dinner partner."

As the limousine arrived at the destination, it lined up behind the other limousines. The driver pulled up into position for photo shoots as each guest exited. The patio of the Wharf brimmed with spring flowers, rivaled only by the twinkling lights set by the Flower Design Depot. Jen felt as if she had stepped into a fairy tale display, as an attendant opened the door of the limousine for them to step out onto the red carpet. Brason got out first and then extended his hand for Jen to exit. JR was the first in the reception line and watched as Jen walked with Brason to his extended hand, greeting them. Jen took his hand and bowed her head with a slight nod as he moved his head close to her cheek, whispering, "You look just like a Miss America…"

Jen smiled and tilted her head with a thank you.

Then JR stood tall, looking to her date. "And you, Brason, how are you tonight?"

"I am perfect tonight, sir."

Jen and Brason passed through the greeting line to find their table. They also passed several tables. The one table Jen was most happy to pass was the staff table where the Angels of Doom sat—all girls, with no dinner partners. She smiled demurely in their direction, only receiving cold stares.

"It is funny how some ill-tempered actions can turn out to have really good results."

"Another moral story?" Brason asked.

"Well, maybe. I believe that a person should commit to project success rather than to do things for personal gain. My interest in the conference was always the work, not the parties. The squad's interest was in block my coming to any party. The moral is that evil actions ricochet back to those committing the evil action—quid pro quo."

"Yes, I understand. I'm really happy that you attended the parties and they didn't get their way. Goodness won the day!"

"I am happy too," Jen said, and Brason tightened his hold on her waist as they reached their table.

The dinner was fabulous, the music was danceable, and Brason was a formidable dance partner. They danced and stayed until they were just about the last few to leave the dance floor. They even hung back to have an aperitif at the bar on the outer deck overlooking the Mystic River. The lights of the Wharf flashed over the water to East Boston, just across the water. It was romantic, as the lights glittered on the water and boats with lighted masts sailed past. Brason and Jen glowed with fascination for each other, and the surroundings enhanced their feelings toward each other.

"Brason, tell me how you got to Harvard and what made you choose the law to reach the level of success you have achieved?"

"First of all, I could not have done it without the support of my loving grandparents. I had a mother and a father who believed the only way for a Negro man to achieve success in the bigoted world they grew up in was for people to get educated, preferably in the law, to affect change. They encouraged me to take full advantage of the programs that were being instituted in the workplace and educational system. It was called affirmative action."

"I'm familiar with it."

"It was a policy that aimed at increasing, among other things, educational opportunities for underrepresented parts of society, implemented by the government. It was set up to overturn historical trends of discrimination against minorities, with grants and scholarships provided by the government. The intent was to foster equality. The policy was also developed to enforce the Civil Rights Act of 1964. It was meant to advance equality, but it is a hard road, and we Blacks must shoulder the burden for the next generations."

"It seems as if our generation must carry the banner for a healthy living environment tomorrow so that the world will be a better place for everyone. We can achieve it only by each one doing the best we can in hopes that at least our United States will be a shining light on the hill."

"Yes, that's exactly right. What are your parents like, Jen?"

"Unfortunately, not at all like yours. My dad will not discuss religion, politics, or unions. He and I are always on opposite sides of the fence. I vote Democrat, and he is a staunch Republican. We argue about the issues rather than discuss their merits or faults. He has fixed ideas about how he wants my life to go, yet never asks how I feel or what I want. He is very difficult. He thinks I won't make it in a man's world. He may be correct, but things are happening in the women's movement through the NOW organization and others to come, I'm certain. I have no time to join anything, but the future holds so much potential and promise for women in the years ahead. What extraordinary things can we achieve in our future? We have a birth control pill that changes a lot of things. How about that?"

"Yes, that has made a great big difference for families, and for women especially, Brown and Black."

"My mom is docile, quiet, and always on Dad's side in appearance, but behind closed doors, she attempts to encourage and support my sister, my brother, or me if she believes in our issue. She tells us that if I cannot change Dad's mind, then I am by his side, though I may not agree with him. *'After all, you children will leave me, and I will be left alone with your father.'*"

"That is a strong barrier to attempt to penetrate."

"It surely is."

"Are you afraid of your parents?"

"No, not afraid. I love them so much it's hard for me to be myself for fear of hurting them. My ideas about a world of justice and equality seem to them like a child's fantasy dream. They say my life has been too easy and that I don't understand the real world. My dad started out very poor, working on the docks without an education. He groveled and worked long, hard hours, yet found a way to become a millionaire. 'Why can't others do the same?' he would ask. He just doesn't see the whole picture."

"It's not quite that easy for everyone, especially those of color. There are so many restrictions and laws that prevent them from getting ahead. After the Reconstruction Act of 1876, which was formed to equalize things, the Confederate states were placed under Union Army governors who enfranchised... gave Blacks the vote...

28

but required them to recite an Oath to the Constitution, effectively discouraging the still-rebellious individuals from voting. This allowed Republican control of many state governments."

"As I see it, many Republicans are without empathy. My father believes in education, but he never allowed me time for relaxation. They had me working at 15 years old after school and on weekends. I grew up with a work ethic that has provided me with an excellent living, and the small $2,000 I saved from the continual gifts of my maternal grandfather, I invested in the purchase of my first house in the country. It came with a large loan from the bank, given to me because the bank handled my dad's company's money and personal money. Few women, especially Black women, were given loans to buy homes in this market. The banks thought women would get pregnant, lose their jobs, and not pay the mortgage—white male supremacy at work. I also applied for scholarships and grants for my education. It has all worked out rather well for me. I will graduate from Suffolk University in May of this year. I want to specialize in Constitutional Law, Civil Rights, or Human Rights. One friend graduated from Suffolk Law in the '50s but was unable to get a job as a lawyer. She became the lead secretary in a law office that had 4 secretaries for five attorneys. I was hesitant about entering law school; however, I saw past the immediate future and into the far tomorrows. The only thing that would make this world a better place, as I see it, is the use of the letter of the law. The law will break barriers. The law is the equalizer for everyone—when the hearts of those judging are honest and fair. Bigotry and hate have strangled the process."

"You sound hopeful but a bit naive, Jen."

"Maybe, but I must be persistent."

"I don't mean to interrupt, but there's the limousine. Let's take it back to the hotel."

"I have an idea. Let's change into comfortable clothes and take a walk around Copley Plaza, and see the lovely window designs of the boutique stores. I'll tell you more about my beautiful city."

"It's a plan. Let's do it."

CHAPTER 6

The ride back to the hotel was charming. Jen and Brason snuggled together and kissed. First, little cheek pecks, and then, in one instant, all the titillation of the week, the togetherness in the Committee, and night's dancing of the fairy princess in her ball gown with Prince Charming in the luxury of their surroundings—both became enraptured with each other. They embraced in a passion that overwhelmed both of them. The extraordinary beauty of the State House, drenched in light, brought Jen back to reality.

She began a nervous chatter again, breaking the spell. "Hey, look. Isn't it beautiful at night?" she said, breaking the intensity of the kiss and substituting the fabulousness of the sight of the gold-domed State House. The dome shone in the night sky like a beacon, telling the city that its leaders were here working for a better future.

"Charles Bulfinch designed the State House, and the city erected it on some part of land bought from the Hancock family. Samuel Adams and Paul Revere laid the cornerstone, which can be seen if you enter the main staircase to the front door. There, you will see it. I often walk up the main staircase in the morning on my way to the office, just for the pleasure of feeling that powerful feeling of oneness with my government. I would turn for one glance east from the front door to see the Park Street Congregational Church, where gunpowder was stored in the basement of that church during the War of 1812, built in 1809. Then I entered and took a glorious walk through time as I dallied through the House of Flags."

"Relax, my dear. You're nervous again. Don't worry. I'm not rushing into anything. I'm quite satisfied with the wonders of your city, but for now, let's just talk about us. Let's tell each other more about what we've done in our lives to get us here. Our time is short until I must leave, only to come back soon," he said, pulling Jen close.

"This is better…" he whispered, pressing the gentlest kiss on her lips. They kissed again, assured that the first passionate kiss would not be the last. They sat snuggled to each other as the limousine arrived at the front door of the hotel. The doorman opened the door, and they exited. They held hands through the lobby, kissed again in the elevator on their ride up, and kissed again as he opened the door to his suite. Once inside, they kissed yet again. The security of his room made the intensity of the kiss more pressing as his body leaned into Jen. They both felt the desire for each other, but neither apparently wanted to create complications so early in their relationship. It already seemed too complicated.

"Did you really mean for us to change and go for a walk for more history?"

"Yes, I meant it. But if you don't want to, I'll understand. However, I will have to change to travel home, since my gown is not comfortable to travel in my 'der Kafer,' better known as 'the Beetle.' But mine I call 'Ghia.' It is the Karmann Ghia, and small."

"Okay, it really sounds like fun, and I love your spontaneity. I'd like to get more comfortable, too."

Jen took her bag into the bathroom, where she had dressed in the gown earlier in the evening. Now, in the early morning of the next day, they were venturing out on a walking tour of her city. It was apparent that neither of them wanted to overstep the boundaries of a proper first date. Jen dressed in brown slacks, a light blue blouse, and a suede jacket with brown leather ankle boots. She took her hair down from its elegant pinning and let it loose around her ears. She was ready for the next phase of getting to know him. One last look in the mirror vanity, a little lipstick to freshen the well-kissed lips, and she was ready.

Brason was looking out the large window in the living room at the center of the square. He really looked Harvard, dressed right out of Brooks Brothers, having discarded the bow tie and tux jacket. He now wore glasses that only enhanced his intellectual demeanor. The handsome couple appeared as though they had stepped off the cover of a fashion magazine. He turned as Jen exited from the bedroom.

"You look like a young schoolgirl… very beautiful, but different than last night."

"You look different, too, but still just as handsome. Only now you look like my college professor for the First Amendment course."

He held out his arms for Jen to be encircled in them. Jen moved into the arms of this extraordinary man. They kissed again, and then he turned back toward the window and asked, "What is that magnificent building?"

"It's the Boston Public Library, established in 1843. It is considered the pioneer of public libraries in America. It was the first large, free municipal library in the United States. It was the first to lend books, the first to have branch libraries, and the first to have a reading room for children. Charles Follen McKim built it. You probably won't have a chance to see the inside, but it is glorious if you ever get a chance. Let's go now, okay?"

"Yes, I will follow you, my personal guide. Is there anything you don't know about Boston?"

"Oh, my heavens, there is so much history to learn. I should study more and become a historian instead of a Civil Rights lawyer."

They laughed and snuggled together on the ride down the elevator. They darted out the side door of the hotel onto Copley Square. The lights were still on in the square since it was about 3:30 a.m., and the Copley Cafeteria had its usual long line waiting for its tantalizing Rubin special sandwich, if one could handle such a food fest so late at night. This was an after-hours hangout for partygoers, open 24 hours a day.

"Come, let's walk up Newbury Street. We'll see Bonwit Teller in its exclusive building, built by W.G. Preston in 1862, free-standing, with valet service and very expensive merchandise. As we walk, I will point out the premier shopping boutiques framed out of the 19th-century brownstone buildings, originally the homes of the very wealthy members of Boston's aristocracy."

"The elegantly decorated storefronts look like Paris," he observed.

"Oh, someday I will go to see the wonders of Paris. They say it is a city for lovers."

"You never can tell. It is on my list of places to see again. Did I mention that my mom was French? Of course, I haven't been there since I was very young, when we went to visit my mom's relatives."

"No. You have not begun to tell me your story. I've usurped the stage."

They walked and talked about their lives, and although he was considered Black, he was rather light-skinned, obviously taken from his mother's side of the gene pool. As they walked, they came upon a bench under a lamppost, where they sat down. Brason began to tell stories of the many horrors of the treatment that he and his family endured for being black and mixed race. So many states forbid interracial marriages, adding jail time and ugliness.

"The ones that suffered the most were generations of my black great-great-grandpappies. They endured unbelievable devastation. My paternal great-great-grandfather and great-grandfather were slaves and came to Tulsa, Oklahoma, from Georgia. Some of my cousins traveled North on the Underground Railroad as fugitives to North Carolina. Freedom was what they all searched for, but freedom comes only in adhering to the rule of law that must be equal for everyone. However, that was not happening. Laws were not on the side of the Blacks. Reconstruction after the Civil War was meant to address the inequities of slavery, to set things straight in its political, social, and economic legacy, and to provide for the reunification of the eleven states that seceded from the Union."

"There are so many false facts we must straighten out, like the one about the Underground Railroad. One story that most people believe is that it was a long underground rail system that went from the South all the way to Boston. *It wasn't.*"

"Well, I suppose the truth is that it did run all the way to Boston, but it was not a railroad with tracks underground, with white railroad conductors who helped the Blacks escape. It wasn't like that at all."

"I suppose some white folks at least helped by giving food and shelter to those who came to their door?"

"I believe that some did, but it was mostly a quiet, secretive underground, somewhat organized by word of mouth in a chain of Black ministers and families who became safe havens for those on their quest to reach freedom under the North Star. The most famous leader was Harriet Tubman. She first found a way for herself; she wanted freedom at any cost. When she was settled in the North, she decided to risk returning in order to bring her husband to freedom. But when she returned for him, she found that he had remarried. She then began to take others willing to endure the hazards of the trek to the North. It was treacherous, from roadway thieves to terrain infested with snakes, wild animals, and all the murdering bigots along the way. The fugitives ran by night and hid by day. The railroad ended in 1865, just before the end of the Civil War and the rise of the Ku Klux Klan. Most of my family's records were destroyed, so I can only listen to my dad's stories, passed down from his father and his father's father. Most old folks don't like to talk about the beatings, the abuse of the men, and the rapes of the women. But we must talk and tell the stories so we know the truth about our past. It hurts the whites…" He stopped mid-sentence, showing hurt in his eyes.

Jen could see that the subject had become far too personal, and that the late, or rather early morning hour, added to the long week of committee meetings, was beginning to show on his tired face.

"My sweet dear, may I suggest that we go back to the suite? It's very late."

"Yes, that is a good idea. Checkout is by 11. My flight back isn't until 3:30 p.m."

"That works. It will give me enough time to take you through the Freedom Trail, if you can tolerate more history of my thrilling city."

"Okay, let's do this. Let's go back to my room, catch a few hours of sleep… promise, only sleep, and then about 10:00 a.m., we will have room service bring us breakfast. I'll pack, and we can be off on your private excursion of your fabulous Freedom Trail."

"Sounds wonderful," Jen happily responded, knowing that sex was not on the program. "After the tour, we can have lunch at my house, if we have time. I will then take you to the airport to catch your flight. Does that sound good?"

"Yes, Jen, it sounds perfect."

Holding hands as they walked, they were both quiet on the walk back to the hotel. The discussion of the past had hurt this gentleman. It was a quiet, secure feeling that there was a reason for their being together. Did they understand the dynamics of their meeting? How would being together affect the lives of each of them? How, then, would their lives affect the lives of their families? The clock had begun, and there was no ability or desire to challenge the future. Destiny had begun. Were they sure this was meant for them? Time would tell, but the moments were now.

In the suite, they took turns in the bathroom, preparing for the few hours' rest they agreed to. Jen changed and returned to Brason, who had slipped into bed and fallen into a much-needed sleep. Jen slid in beside him and put her arms around his waist as he turned to tuck Jen into himself in a spooning form to sleep.

Brason kissed Jen's cheek, head, and back, with tender kisses, assuring her that tomorrow would be another fabulous day. They slept as the talk of the agonies of the past slipped away into hopes and dreams of tomorrow.

CHAPTER 7

They both woke to the soft chimes of the travel clock Brason had set for 9 a.m. The two ruffled around in the sheets until they were facing each other. They kissed. The magic lingered from the night before, and the morning desire was still as strong, but so was their desire to keep it 'fresh and light.'

"If you would like to shower, you may go first, and I will order us breakfast from Room Service."

"Okay. That is perfect." Jen grabbed her overnight bag and headed for the shower.

"Is a vegetable omelet with Swiss cheese okay?" he yelled to Jen in the shower.

"Sounds delicious." Jen dried off, applied body cream, as always, and ran a comb through her hair. She came out in the outfit she had worn for the night walk.

"You look great," he said, looking up from reading the Boston newspaper delivered to each room every morning. "I guess we made some news last night. I never had the chance to tell you, though I haven't formally announced it… I will run for governor in the next election. I have the necessary signatures that allow me to run. With that, the papers are always tracking news and that, at the moment, is us."

"What does that mean by 'us'?"

"It only means now that there will be a lot of questions as to who you are. What are we doing together? Is this a serious relationship?

How will a single Black man running for office handle all the racial challenges of a mixed relationship? How will it affect the voting? Will I hold the Black votes? Will I get the vote of some white folks?"

"Oh my gosh, that's a lot of pressure to begin a relationship on, isn't it?"

"It certainly is. Which is why I said at the beginning I had no time for mistakes. I don't think that we are a mistake, but I don't want to pressure you. That is precisely why I think we should hold off any intimacy until we have a sure mind as to what is ahead for both of us. I believe in love at first sight."

"Boy, first thing in the morning, you certainly hit a girl with complex options… Should I stay or should I go? Should I run away?" Jen asked.

Brason stepped into the shower, yelling back. "No, don't run away. Wait. This will only take a few moments."

A knock on the door brought Jen back to present reality. She opened it to a waiter wheeling in breakfast. He set it before the large window, where they could see the path journeyed together the night before, talking about the past and their families.

"Breakfast is served. It looks delicious."

"I'll be right there." He soon was.

Breakfast was delicious, just as it looked. They ate in silence, giving weight to the air in this lovely room.

"This omelet is absolutely heavenly. I cannot believe that I was this hungry."

"I think we talked and danced so much that we hardly ate our dinner."

It was 'small talk' to avoid anything serious. They finished. Everything was packed, and they checked the room so nothing would be left behind. They closed the door to their night's sleep together.

"I'll go to the front desk to close my bill."

"Okay, I'll go get my car and meet you in the front—no, not a good idea? Do you think there might be reporters waiting?"

"Could be, so why don't I meet you down in the parking garage at your car? That way, no one knows you or your car. Is that okay? Sorry to be so clandestine."

"Of course. I'll wait for you in my car." They left in opposite directions only to meet again in a few moments. Within a short time, he was there.

"Let's go!" He directed as he knocked on the window of the driver's side. Jen released the lock on the trunk where he placed his luggage, then hopped into the passenger side. "We're off to another tour by Jen," he enthusiastically announced. They both smiled a warm, caring smile at each other.

"Yes, we are off on the Freedom Trail through the towns I loved most in life. I don't want to take the overpasses. I want to take us through the towns, hoping to see them as they are today and tell you how they were years ago. My intention is to truly take you, my new friend, along the true path of the Freedom Trail." She drove out of the garage and headed up Beacon Hill, where the State House sits.

"As we go, I will drive through the center of downtown, explaining everything as we pass, but most of what we will pass is best done on foot—someday, when you have time. Not today. For now, I will point out the various attractions as we pass.

"I guess you recognize that majestic gold-domed Boston State House, circa 1795, on your left and the Boston Common to the right. As we pass down the side, we will see a portion of the Granary Burying Ground, circa 1660. It is the resting place of three of the signers of the Declaration of Independence: John Hancock, Robert Treat Paine, and Samuel Adams. Later, Paul Revere, Benjamin Franklin's parents, and the victims of the Boston Massacre found their resting places as well.

"Going through the banking district, we will come out near the Old South Meeting House, built in 1729 as a Puritan meeting house where the Boston Tea Party began. Then there is the Old State House, Boston's oldest public building (1713), and across from it are the cobblestones marking the site where British soldiers at the start of the Boston Massacre killed five Americans.

"Faneuil Hall marketplace, donated to the city in 1742 by Peter Faneuil, was and still is a marketplace on the first floor and a meeting hall on the second floor, called the 'Cradle of American Liberty' by Marquis de Lafayette.

"As we travel down Hanover Street, this is the Little Italy of the neighborhood. The shops we pass along the way are mostly family-owned, and when we take a right down this narrow street, it ends at the house of Paul Revere, built in 1680. It is the oldest wooden structure still standing, at 19 North Square. Paul Revere owned the house from 1770 to 1800. This home is where he left to go down to the docks for a boat to cross the river to Charlestown, where he could easily see the Old North Church Tower for the signal to begin his 'midnight ride.'

"If I turn up the next street, it gets us back onto Hanover, and turning right, we will see the backside of the Old North Church, built in 1723. On April 18, 1775, it was agreed that should the British troops begin their march, a signal would be mounted in the steeple of the Christ Church showing lanterns 'one if by land, two if by sea.'

"Eagerly waiting on the Boston shore was Paul Revere, while William Dawes, saddled up and ready to ride, waited on the shore. Later, they met up with Samuel Prescott. Two lamps showed: Paul Revere pulled on the reins—and it was off to Lexington—and Concord to warn John Hancock and Samuel Adams of the advancing British army. Dawes, in like fashion, went off in the opposite direction, going through Roxbury.

"The men feared being captured before warning Hancock and Adams that the British troops were on the way. The three men, Revere, Dawes, and Prescott, met up in Lexington and were, in fact, captured after leaving Lexington on the way to Concord shortly after midnight. Dawes and Prescott escaped. Revere did not. The British, however, released him in a short time, but claimed his horse.

"The colonists were warned. Yet Paul Revere feared British Redcoats would take all the weapons stored in Concord; they did not. The colonists along the way heard the cry, 'The British are coming!' But those words, some say, were never shouted out by Paul Revere in the early morning hours of April 19, 1775."

"Did he ride quietly? Maybe he did both."

"He rode on horse quickly and yet quietly, signaling colonists along the river, heading from Charlestown on the evening of April 18, 1775. New England soldiers faced the British army for the first time in a bloody battle on a 'hilly landscape of fenced pastures' situated across the Charles River from Boston. Casualties were heavy for the British, inflicted by the provincial soldiers from Massachusetts, Connecticut, and New Hampshire. Fifty years after the battle, Marquis de Lafayette set the cornerstone of a 221-foot obelisk built from quarried granite in a lasting monument to the memory of the Battle of Bunker Hill—the battle known as Breed's Hill. There it is just ahead and to your left.

"How are you doing? Have you had enough history yet?"

"I'm doing just fine. Are you tired yet?"

"No. I'm still so excited about being with you that it hasn't hit me yet." Jen turned onto a road along the path through Somerville and into Medford with the Mystic River to their right. She pointed out the boat route and where Revere actually could see the church steeple.

"All this is built up, but it was all farmland in its time."

"Yes: no transportation, only carriage and horse paths that were made by travelers and scouts, furrowing out new areas to develop."

"I suppose that river also provided supplies to the troops at Lexington and Concord?"

"Yes, I guess that's right. Boats still go from small lakes converging on the river even today. The boats will travel from Medford, where today there is a Boat Club for members, some with motor boats on the lower lake and others with sailboats on the upper lake. Of course, the lower lake is approachable from downriver, and one can reach the river behind the Wharf restaurant that empties out into the Atlantic Ocean."

"It's getting late, and I'm not certain we will be able to get through the Lexington and Concord Battle. However, if we make a convenient stop, I will… maybe change my flight schedule. What say you, Miss Tour Guide?"

"I was thinking the same thing. We are very close to the Buckman Tavern in Lexington. It is a structure listed as the oldest tavern in Lexington, circa 1704-1710. A historic Revolutionary War Site, associated with the first battle of Lexington and Concord. We could stop, and you can call to change your ticket."

"Good idea. What should I change it to?"

"My weekend is free. I planned to rest, relax, and maybe take a horseback ride through the apple orchard in back of my house. What does your weekend look like?"

"Well, I was planning to do somewhat the same, except that once I'm home, I will be riddled with phone calls."

"Would you like to hide out at my little cottage in the country for an extra day?"

"Sounds intriguing. Yes, I'd love that."

They arrived at the Tavern, and its attention to historic detail was impressive. Jen was directed to a table, and Brason found a telephone. When Brason returned, he sat and said, "I have arranged to stay one more night and to take the 2:30 flight out on Sunday. I hope that fits into your plans?"

"Oh, Brason, that sounds just right. Did you notice I did not say 'perfect?' Everything so far has been just 'perfect.' It is becoming redundant. Now, we can relax and have a cup of tea, coffee, or hot chocolate and enjoy Lexington."

The waitress came to us, "Is this your first time in the Tavern?"

"Yes, for both of us," Brason said.

She gave a brief history. "It was used as a meeting place for town meetings by Captain Parker and his militia. Then, on the early morning of April 19, 1775, he sat in the Tavern to await the arrival of the Redcoats. That would be the beginning of the Lexington and Concord Battle. It was also a place for travelers to spend a night during their travels," she told us.

"What will you have?"

"We will both have Earl Grey tea," Brason said, "that is, if you have it?" They both laughed, remembering that tea was a very important factor in the American Revolution—The Boston Tea Party.

"Yes, we do have it, but just a side note, it originated in 1830 by Lord Grey, a partner at Robert Jackson & Co." She headed for the kitchen to fill the order.

"I am so happy that you decided to stay a bit longer. I was dreading our having to rush through all the things I was hoping to show you. Now we can take our time."

"I'm happy too."

With tea finished, they walked around the gardens. The green showed no outward sign of the battles fought here.

"If I listen very closely, I might hear the cries of those militiamen whose lives lie in the history of this land."

"It was a lovely spring day, and Brason must have had enough history by now." Jen wanted to get to her house in the country so they might take a horseback ride through the apple orchard and then relax.

"The tea has refreshed us and satisfied our appetite for any food, and we are still filled from our delicious breakfast. We can wait until we get to your house to have a candlelight dinner."

"I certainly have two lobster tails in the freezer that would make a delicious dinner, with baked potato and string beans," Jen said. "Interesting how that word 'perfect' seems to be the only word to use, and it fits so often. Here it is again. 'Perfect!' So, now it's time for us to leave the history of Lexington and Concord behind and go to my home. There is not much history in my house, but I am making history in my neighborhood because I am a single woman, living in a house by herself, with no husband in sight and no father or mother to share it with. My neighbor was speechless when she came to greet me, my husband, or maybe my mom and dad, when all she found was me. I was alone in a three-bedroom house on an acre of land with a two-stall barn. It flipped out my neighbor."

"Where is your husband?" she asked.

"Oh, I don't have a husband. I am not married."

"Yes, of course. You live with your mother and father." It was more a statement than a question.

"No, they live a few towns east of here."

She was speechless.

"I suppose you will flip them out again when they see you with a Black guy? Will they give you trouble?"

"Yes, I suppose they might not like a Black in the neighborhood, but if we are going to do this, we are going to have to talk, not only to neighbors but moms, dads, aunts, uncles, and the likes on both sides. If we take this any further, how will all of them on both sides take to 'us'?"

The question hung in the air. They talked only about the beauty of the landscape on the roads from Lexington to Jen's home close to New Hampshire. As the two approached the white house with blue trim, it was evident that the gardeners had been there. The mowed lawn looked lush and green for the weekend. Jen was always happy when they did that. The trees were in bloom, as were the flowers in the beds around the house. The remaining lawn, groomed and plush, stretched to the barn at the far edge of the property, leading to the orchard.

"That's a good-looking house. How long have you owned it?"

"I bought it a few years ago, just before I started working for the AG. I really hate to pay rent. At the end of a year, all I have is a bunch of receipts. When you own it, each payment builds equity."

"You're so smart and wise for such a little thing. What are you, about five feet?"

"Actually, I'm five feet one inch, to be exact." She emphasized the inch.

"Okay, I guess that extra inch makes a difference."

"Yes, an inch makes a difference to me."

They laughed as they got out of the car and approached the side entrance that brought them into the breezeway, which connected the main house to the garage. It had been turned into another paneled room, which Jen uses as an office, den, and additional guest room. Jen unlocked the sliding glass doors that brought them into the kitchen. She turned to face Brason and said, "Welcome to my home."

"It is truly a charming home."

"I'll show you around, and then you can get your luggage and set up in the guest room next to my room." She walked him down the hall, pointing out the mini guest room, which she uses as a dressing room, the guest room, and then the master bedroom with its king-sized bed.

"That's some bed?"

"Yes, I needed the space when I had my German Shepherd and two poodles."

"Where are they now?"

"Life has a way of changing things, and new decisions must be made. I loved having my animals, but sometimes love doesn't take care of the problem. I had to give them up for adoption. I work so many hours. I could not leave them alone for all those hours. My dad took one poodle, and my brother and his wife took the other. The Shepherd went back to its original owner, who was German. The dog knew only German commands."

"How did you command it?"

"In German, of course. I learned the few commands that were necessary, and she and I got along really well." Jen moved into the lovely, cozy, fireplace living room with its large picture window looking out to the front lawn.

"This is so nice. Can we build a fire?"

"Yes, of course. Here is where I usually spend New Year's Eve celebration alone."

"Why alone?"

"It's a special night, and being alone with a plate of spaghetti and meatballs, with a crackling fire and watching the crazy crowds in New York City suits me just fine."

"Isn't it lonely?"

"No, it's a whole lot lonelier being with a crowd of people drinking and partying with no one special to share it with. I'm safer and happier right here in this wonderful room."

"I can see this is the dining room. That is a lovely little crystal chandelier over a round dining table. I like round tables. Conversation is so much easier."

"Yes, I agree. I love my house. I even installed that chandelier myself. Of course, I could have electrocuted myself because when the man at the store told me how to hang it, he forgot to tell me I had to turn off the electricity."

"So, you hung it with the electricity on?"

"Yup… but here I am, and there it is."

"Pretty cool, kid."

"Would you like to see the back yard?" She guided him through the foyer and out the door to the back, where they walked hand in hand to the barn.

"The horses have been brushed and fed," Teddy, the owner of the horses, told them. Jen introduced him to Brason.

They shook hands, and Teddy asked, "Jen, would you and your friend like to take a ride? The horses are ready, if you want to?"

"We've had a very busy week. Mr. Washington is the Attorney General of his state and has been working in our State House for the entire week at a conference."

"Sounds deep. So, feel free to take the horses out for a ride. I'm going home."

"Thanks, Teddy. I think we will take a very short ride through the apple orchard, but I'm not certain. The day is so fresh and New England-ish… if there is such a word." Everyone laughed.

Teddy lived next door, so he simply went from Jen's backyard to his home. Jen and Brason walked back to the house through the breezeway and out the front door to the car to get the luggage. Brason brought his bags into the guest room, and Jen brought hers to her room. She took fresh towels out of the linen closet and brought them to Brason.

"Here are your towels. The sheets are clean on this bed, so please make yourself comfortable. I'm changing into jeans for our ride. Do you still wish to do that?"

"Actually, I'd like to leave that for another time in our lives, if that is agreeable with you?"

"No problem. Let's get into comfortable clothes. After which, I will open a nice bottle of wine, and we can sit in the living room. I'll put some music on for us to relax and enjoy the fire and our time together."

"That sounds perfect. It's as if we are lost in space and time, with no one who knows where we are or that we are together."

"You mean, no one to cast judgment on us?"

"Maybe, but rather like we are suspended in time and space—just us, alone with each other."

Brason followed Jen into the kitchen, where he helped open a bottle of Merlot while Jen prepared some cheese and crackers to hold them until dinnertime.

She took out two crystal glasses, and Brason poured wine into each glass, filling them slightly less than halfway. They took the glasses, the bottle, and the tray of cheese into the living room, where Jen lit a log and started the fireplace.

"A toast to you, my beautiful new friend," he said.

"And to you, too. It feels remarkably right, but…"

"No buts. 'I'd call it perfect.'" They both laughed at that word again.

They settled in for an extraordinary evening together. They moved from the sofa to the throw pillows Jen had strategically placed near the fireplace for her to lie before the fireplace on cool nights. In New England, spring may very well bring snow and sometimes even a squall. They lounged on the floor, with the pillows to support them, the fire to warm them, and the wine to arouse the sexual desire building between them.

"It is such a joy to be here with you, getting to know who you are, and being free to make judgments for ourselves."

"While we are on the subject of getting to know each other, I have not told you all about myself, but I would like to leave all that for dinner. Right now, I want you for myself." He moved close to her as passion swelled inside them. They kissed with greater passion than even those of yesterday evening.

CHAPTER 8

8

The logs burned low, the stereo music stopped, and Jen and Brason woke in each other's arms, happy to be together. The stress of the week and the newness of the relationship found peace in the relaxed manner of the moment.

"Well, that was a well-needed nap for both of us," he said as he gathered himself to an upright position.

The sun was setting, and the night's cold air made it necessary to place more logs on the fire and possibly to turn on the heat just to take the chill out of the house.

"I offer you the dinner menu. You have a choice of New England lobster tail with baked potato and a vegetable, with clam chowder as a starter, or filet mignon with the same sides, minus the clam chowder."

"Since we had the roast beef for dinner last night, I think I would like to have the lobster dinner with the clam chowder."

"Great, let's get it going. I can't believe I am hungry again."

"Actually, I am hungry too. If we think about it, we haven't eaten since breakfast except for the crackers and cheese."

"You're right. So, let's get to it."

"What can I do to help?"

"I love it. You are willing to help in the kitchen?"

"Yes, of course. I even cook when we are having a family gathering. I will spend two days preparing my ham hocks and beans. The process takes two days if you want to get them right."

"Will you cook for me one day?"

"Absolutely. I'll even wash the dishes with you. I'll go shopping with you. I will do everything with you. I will even change the baby's diapers."

"Whoa. That was a fast and steady move from washing dishes to having children."

"Ya, I guess we have a lot to talk about at dinner," he murmured as he kissed the back of Jen's neck while she snuggled into his kiss.

"Okay, you can start by setting the table with the good dishes."

"Do you have bad dishes? I certainly don't want to eat on bad dishes."

"Well, I have dishes for everyday use and dishes for special occasions, like Thanksgiving and Christmas, and *you*. The very best I have for a very special man." She planted a kiss on his cheek. "While I get the food, would you get another bottle of wine?"

"Since we are having fish, I think I'll take this bottle of Pinot Grigio, if it is okay?"

"Yes, it is exactly what I would have chosen, but it should be slightly chilled."

"Should I put it in the freezer for a few moments?"

"That's good. Have you noticed I haven't said that word?"

"Oh, you mean that word that seems to be us every time?"

"Yes."

"… but it is… PERFECT…" Both blurted out the word and kissed at the end.

"Yes, to all of it," she replied, continuing her preparations in the kitchen as he hovered around her, talking about his life.

"Have you ever heard of the Tulsa Massacre?"

"Let me think, Tulsa? Didn't it take place in Oklahoma?… That's about all I know about it."

"Yes, it was in Oklahoma. My great-granddad and granddad were leaders of the state's second-largest African American community in Tulsa in the early '20s. It was a residential neighborhood called Greenwood, where my great-granddad and my granddad owned a tailor shop in one of the country's most prosperous Black communities. It was also known as the Black Wall Street Market. On May 31, 1921, white mobs assailed and plundered this peaceful neighborhood. Within sixteen hours, thirty-five square blocks were torched, burned, and leveled by a fire that burned until the next day of June 1. A hateful white mob stripped an undetermined amount of Black wealth from future generations."

"I'm so sorry. As a white person, I feel ashamed, though my grandparents came from Italy, and somehow that seems different. I am from an immigrant family, but the thought hurts me on both sides. I've been called a Guinea Nigger, pardon the expression."

"Nigger? Why would anyone call you a nigger?"

"It goes back to the 1740s, and by the 1840s, the term referred to Italians from the south of Italy, in Sicily. Those Sicilians were darker than the Northern Italians. So, as a result of name-calling, I got to know the feeling of discrimination a little, but not as badly as you."

"Well, probably not… but now, back to the massacre. It wasn't only the Black Wall Street Massacre that diminished the wealth of Black businesses. But, now, for a little bit of a history lesson… Massacres happened in New York in 1863; Memphis and New Orleans in 1866; Wilmington, N.C., in 1898; then in Atlanta in 1906; Springfield in 1908; East St. Louis in 1917; Chicago in 1919; and Rosewood, Florida, in 1923, along with others I don't want to get into. They were all mass killings. Mobs of whites killing Blacks."

"Oh, Brason, that is so painful for me to hear. Humans are killing humans for nothing other than the color of their skin. Destroying precious lives. It must be brutal for you to endure."

"Yes, it is hurtful to think about, but we must expose it all in order to destroy it and never allow it to happen again. We must learn history so as not to repeat the same errors."

"It is similar to that of the parents of Italians from the North who didn't want their sons or daughters to marry Sicilians because of their dark color and their bad name. When the Mafia became known, people were afraid of those Sicilian families. No one could tell that we were Sicilian if we didn't tell them. No one would know, since we are all quite light-skinned, as you can see. However, I do recall when the riots began, I was very thankful that the color of my skin was not brown or black. Some Sicilians are quite dark brown, with kinky hair, as some of my cousins."

"Yes, you can understand, and maybe you can empathize with how deeply agonizing it is for me to know that so many Blacks have suffered in these massacres, and yet to this day, few Blacks or whites know much about them."

(The ping from the timer sounded.)

"The wine is ready."

"Should I open one bottle?"

"Of course. I like history lessons with wine," she said, trying to ease a bit of the pain that both of them felt by this time. "How did the massacre in Tulsa happen?"

"So stupid," he began. "A tall, skinny, velvet-skinned Black nineteen-year-old teenage star football player who had dropped out of school because he was making a lot of money shining the shoes of oil men in the city created the story. The kid's name was Dick Rowland. It was May 30, 1921. Rowland took a break from his shoe stand in the pool hall, heading for the only building in the area that allowed a public restroom for Blacks. Tulsa was segregated, of course. After he was done, Rowland returned and stepped into a wire-caged elevator going down, driven by a 17-year-old white girl, Sarah Page. No one knew that they were very good friends. Vague reports exist of his trip down in the elevator, except that possibly the elevator jolted, and Rowland stepped on the girl's foot or bumped into her, causing her to let out a loud scream. By the time they reached the bottom, and as soon as the gate opened, Rowland ran like the wind, knowing what could happen."

"Did they catch him?"

"Yes, the police caught him, arrested him, and the mobs were ready to lynch him when the girl confessed that it was an accident and that nothing had happened between them. However, the Tulsa Tribune's headlines read: 'Nigger attacks girl in elevator.' Three hours after the Tulsa Tribune papers hit the streets, the massacre began… the burning of Black Wall Street and the millions of Black men's dollars burned to the ground. The lynch mob took Rowland, dragged him, and did what they did best: strung him up to die. The police brutality was too much to talk about then and is still unbearable to think about now. The Tulsa Race Massacre is considered the single most horrific incident of racial terrorism since slavery. We all managed to get through the slave owners' years of destroying Black men's dignity and perseverance while they continually raped our women. However, through all this, resentment is not easily changed to acceptance with forgiveness. Forgiveness can only come with the true belief, as Lincoln believed, that the distinctive trait of our republic is that it was 'conceived in liberty and dedication to the proposition that all men are created equal' by the principles of its original democratic belief. The United States has always been looked upon as the world's major experiment in democracy."

"Democracy is an ideal—simple but complex—and can only function when good and honorable men and women perform their duties with good and honorable deeds for all people, especially those in government positions."

(The timer rings—again.)

"Dinner must be ready. I heard the timer. Let's put aside the world's problems for now."

"Sounds good. The lobster is baked, judging from the timer, and it is time for a little Debussy with dinner. While I change the music, please sit and pour us wine for a toast."

Jen filled the soup tureen with the hot clam chowder. She covered it and placed it on the table. Then she decorated the dinner plates with fresh parsley, a baked lobster tail, a roasted potato, and baby broccoli sprigs. She placed everything on the table so as not to get up until dessert. Brason had rinsed the wine glasses and readied them for the Pinot.

"Here we are," he said, handing Jen her glass and lifting his.

"What shall we toast to?"

"First, I would like to toast to the accomplishments of my new friend, Jen… an extraordinary woman that I hope to have in my life for a long time, one way or another."

"I toast to the magnificent man who has come into my life, and I pray will be here for an exhilarating future."

(Each took a sip of wine.)

"Let us pray in thanks for this moment together and the delicious food."

"Of course, and let's ask for guidance as to where and how we can make a significant difference in this world with so much hurt and obvious discord."

Throughout dinner, the two talked freely about how each of them had grown up. He explained that through his church, many organizations had assisted him in reaching his many achievements. Then, with a heart filled with sadness balanced by a whole lot of pride, he extolled the story of his French Catholic mother and Southern Baptist father.

"Well, my mother and Dad met at the University of Virginia. They worked together to establish chapters for the New Negro Alliance (NNA) for equality in hiring within the food industry throughout the country.

This movement began in Chicago, Harlem, and Washington in 1933. Mom would prepare flyers and packets for Dad to distribute in all the small southern towns. The movement against the food industry, such as the Stop & Shop, Piggly Wiggly, the Thompson Company restaurant chain, General Foods, and Chock Full o'Nuts, proved successful but slow-moving."

"I guess no one realized how extensive and important the food market was to the financial benefits of these companies by the African Americans purchasers."

"You're right. However, once the movement began to see its success, more and more people joined the organization. In 1933, when Dad began with the NNA, there were only 300 members. One year later, after Dad visited the many small southern towns, the membership, campaigns, together with the successful boycotts had increased to 140,000. My dad was a major factor in its successful development. The movement targeted Woolworth's Five-and-Dime stores, which refused to employ Blacks as counter clerks. Leaders called for Black solidarity 'to break the backs of one of the largest white-owned companies in the city.' It forced the companies to comply with the demands for equality, or suffer the losses."

"I remember reading that when Rosa Parks sat down, the movement stood up and stopped riding the buses. It hit the pocketbooks of the businesses. That always gets their attention," Jen contributed.

"These successful movements brought some balance, but not enough, as the Blacks continued their fight. What it did bring throughout the South was a number of angry whites attacking travelers as they moved from the South to northern states, whether for business or personal reasons. Lynching seemed to become the punishment for Blacks and Jews by self-elected white vigilantes."

"Didn't that make it very dangerous for your dad?"

"After establishing a new group, Dad called Mom and me to say he was beginning his travel back home and would see us in a day or two. But Dad never came home."

"Oh, no! What happened?"

"I was 4 years old when the phone rang and a member of the NNA told Mom that a lynch mob had stopped Dad and his partner on the road through Arkansas on his way home. They set up a Kangaroo Court and found them both guilty and hanged them, leaving them there to be eaten by the animals, birds, bugs, and whatever. When Dad did not call the NNA that evening, the local church went to pick up the bodies and send them home."

"Your mom must have been devastated."

"Mom hung up the line of the phone and began to cry. But at four, I could only ask her if she was, 'Okay, mom?' It was never okay after that."

"What did you do then?"

"Mom had some friends in North Carolina, where the conflict had not reached in such large measure. So we went there, and Mom taught school while I attended an Episcopal preschool."

"Well, life got better then, right?"

"Wrong. Life became very difficult, and the icy cold winter became a terribly bad year for us. Mom caught pneumonia and was never able to get back to her healthy self. The loss of my dad also contributed to her depression and demise. She died at twenty-five years old. I was six years old when I went to live with Grandpa and Grandma Washington in Oklahoma. I grew healthy and strong. I went to school and listened well to Grandma. I had a very supportive group of family and friends.

"When I grew up, my grandfather took me to Alabama on a Freedom Bus to the hallowed ground of the civil rights struggle. We took a bus to march at the Edmund Pettus Bridge in Tulsa, Oklahoma, to meet Martin Luther King and John Lewis on a peaceful march, which became known as 'Bloody Sunday.' The peaceful demonstration turned into five days of beatings, bloodshed, and death.

"As the marchers walked in twos over the Bridge, we could see the line at the end of the bridge where police stood creating a human wall with clubs in their hands and wearing masks to protect themselves from the potential flood of tear gas that would be blown into the atmosphere where peaceful demonstrators walked. They organized a vigilante group riding horses under the command of Maj. John Cloud, who ordered the marchers to disperse. When they did not, he directed that gas canisters be thrown into the crowds. As soon as that took place, it seemed that all hell broke loose as the troopers beat everyone close enough to them. The gas choked the demonstrators as they turned to go back to where Hosea Williams, John Lewis, Albert Turner, and Bob Mants, along with hundreds of non-violent activists, had begun the walk at the Brown Chapel.

"During the upheaval of that peaceful demonstration, men and women were beaten so badly that by the time someone was able to get the injured to a hospital 20 miles away, many died. The police pushed us back over the bridge."

"I thought that your family had lost everything in the Tulsa massacre?"

"Yes, they did, but they were also very knowledgeable businessmen. They had insurance, of course; however, for insurance purposes, the Tulsa Massacre was referred to as a 'race massacre,' thereby releasing the insurance companies from paying what people had in insurance. The companies felt they didn't have to pay since it was a race thing and not a reliable insurance factor. My family fought it and won. The money provided, along with their other investments, allowed them to rebuild their business and continue to grow. I grew up, and they helped me through college. I did all the wonderful things that led me to an elected office. My family is composed of marvelous people. They will love you."

"And I'm certain I will love them back."

CHAPTER 9

Brason's expression showed the combination of pain, balanced by acceptance, as he continued his story at dinner.

"I was sent to Tulsa after Mom died. Both Dad and Mom are buried there in our family plot. Grandfather's house was warm and comfortable, and I grew strong with love and encouragement. My Grandmother is a severely critical woman who keeps a fastidious house and expects everyone to do the same. My great-grandfather, vibrant but old, still lived with his son, my paternal grandfather, and Grandma became my surrogate mother through the years. She watched over me with strict love, giving me lessons on living life to its fullest each day, just as she had done while Mom and Dad were alive, supporting the NNA, Freedom Rides, and fighting for civil rights and voting rights.

"Lots of learning often comes from our grandparents, just as in my life," Jen interjected.

"Which grandparents?"

"Well, my maternal grandfather lives with my dad and mom. I love him so. He is so real, honest, and true to reality. If I am confused about life, he is the one I go to because he sets out all the varying possibilities with good answers, resulting in wise decisions. He should have been an attorney, but he was a contractor, ran his own company, and did concrete work for the City of Boston."

"He sounds like someone I want to meet."

"If you decide to see me again after you return home," Jen teased, "and if I decide I want to see you again," she continued the tease, "I trust you both will meet, and you will love him."

Brason reached for her hand and kissed the top. "I will want to see you each day from now on, but it will not be easy. You will have to be the decision-maker as we move forward. I have one more year as Attorney General, and then I will make a run for Governor."

"I graduate in May next year and take my bar exam in July or February of the next year, since Massachusetts only offers the bar exam at those times."

"Then you can help me with the final months of my campaign to win in November."

"That seems so far away, and there are so many issues, but if we can go steadily and speed ahead, we can become really good friends and possibly lovers for life."

"Jen, I told you that I didn't want to make any mistakes. I have so many plans that must fit right for me to accomplish all I want. You are someone who has unexpectedly come into my life; I was never looking for you. However, there you are. Once that happened, all things seemed to move differently. Sooooo, here we sit, sipping wine, eating lobster tail, and loving being here together. Just us, safe in our 'bubble'."

"I think we must take each day as it appears and ask God to watch over us and guide us in the work that we want to do. We must walk through the obstacle course ahead. If all that is agreeable, then the only challengers will be with our families and the world, both objecting to interracial unions."

"We will cross those bridges as we get to them. Let us take each item as a separate unit and solve them as we go. Okay?"

"Yes, but I am extremely frightened of the future in our world and all that we will face with our families and our careers."

"I've been afraid in my life, but as long as I know what I want, what I must do to achieve it, and commit to it, then I know I can fulfill it. I'm not afraid!" Brason bravely responded.

"Is that how we will achieve our dreams?"

"Yes. It will not be easy. It's never been easy, but I know I can do it. I hope you will be willing to do it with me."

By this time, Jen and Brason had discussed a plethora of circumstances they would face. With dinner finished, it was time for dessert. Coffee was ready.

"Let's move into the living room. I'll put another log on the fire," she said, leading him into the living room. "Please, pour a snifter glass with an ounce of Grand Marnier Cordon Rouge. It is an orange-flavored liqueur created in 1880 by Alexandre Marnier-Lapostolle. It is Cognac brandy, distilled essence of bitter orange, and sugar. Take small sips to savor the taste. It is also a digestive. You'll love it."

Brason went to the small serving bar, which held the Cognac. He poured two snifter glasses of Grand Marnier. He handed one glass to Jen as she finished placing a new log on the fire. They sat again on the large, comfortable cushions near the fire. Both were sufficiently satisfied with their meal, and now this after-dinner drink was a new experience for Brason as he savored the delicious flavor of the Grand Marnier.

"A toast to you, my precious Jen. I hope I haven't frightened you away with my life and my calculated dreams. My hope is that you will consider being with me through it all as my partner, if all goes well, but certainly as my very best friend, anyway."

"I will drink to all of that."

"I see your piano, so with my unusual perceptive powers, I've determined it is you who must play it. Am I wrong?"

"No, you are right. Although I am not nearly as well-practiced as I was before law school. I can still play a few classical pieces. What I do like is to play my piano-bar style music. Would you like to hear something?"

"Yes, what a treat. What don't you do?"

"Lots, my dear."

He settled in among the floor cushions as Jen got up to the piano. After a few movements of Beethoven's Moonlight Sonata, she turned to play and sing Jacques Brel's If You Go Away? (She finished.)

"Wow, I'm moved. That was absolutely amazing. I'm overwhelmed," he said, rising from the cushions and going to her.

She stood to face him as he kissed her with a deep but gentle kiss. Before separating, he said, "I will only go away if you want me to, but if I stay, I will make it a day like no day has been nor will be again, I promise you." He repeated the words of the song. He kissed her, and they kissed until the passion that had blossomed between them during their week of work together had become unharnessed, and they reached for each other in total abandonment.

The two lovers moved toward the king-size bed. Each gently removed the other's clothing until they stood naked before each other.

The heat from each other's bodies encircled the lovers as they lay on the clean, white sheets.

"You are so beautiful!" he remarked, "so smooth, like white satin." He caressed her breasts and kissed her nipples.

"You are handsome… smooth like black velvet," she whispered as she ran her hands along his well-developed chest, followed by kisses as her hands passed over his body.

Brason gathered her face in his hands and pressed a full mouth kiss that gently opened her lips to his searching tongue. They pushed into each other's bodies as the arousal of his power surfaced in search of the love that he sought to find, and she ached to let him have. They melted into a cuddle, entangled together with the black velvet skin of Brason on the silken white skin of Jen, an amalgamation of two cultures that was forbidden, abhorred and illegal in many states. Together, nothing from outside was evident in this room. Here, only two people existed, who had unexpectedly found each other. For now, all they wanted was each other. Only they existed at this moment in time. They chose this relationship; now they would have to face the ugliness of the world. All that must be decided as they move forward. However, they will face it together tomorrow.

They made love with such tenderness, each for the first time, and with each other.

He kissed her mouth with passion that swept down his body through his loins as he felt the heat from her body pushing into his. He moved his kisses from her neck and kissed his way to the taut nipple, seeking his wet lips. The kiss peaked with excitement in Jen's eager folds, her hidden lips reaching for him. The strength of his need was ready to satisfy her anxious, hungry body. However, there was so much more area that Brason wanted to nibble and kiss. Brason continued kissing Jen down the center of her stomach, stopping to kiss the left nipple that begged for its attention. Jen was wiggling with desire for more.

"Relax, my sweet, there is no reason to rush this precious moment. Just feel the energy and heat between us and let it fill your entire body with the excitement and joy I am feeling."

"I am feeling the same," Jen replied, but she did not want to tell him that she was having trouble controlling the urge to rush to her climax. "I have little experience in this type of lovemaking."

Brason silenced her with a passionate kiss on her lips while moving his fingers to the juices that flowed in her body as he searched for the warm, heated fluid of her loving, as she stretched her body in pure ecstasy. With relaxed sensuality, Brason massaged the area. "We can take all the time we need to enjoy this journey, never before traveled."

Jen slid her position down to place a kiss on his manhood, swishing her tongue around the tip, sending Brason into moans that excited Jen even more. She moved her body so that together they made love to each other until the heat of their kissing caused each body part to cry out for the ultimate. As Brason raised his body over Jen's, they looked into each other's eyes with loving anticipation as Brason's aching throb filled her softness and entered with fulfillment, allowing each to see the pleasure on the other's face as she brought her hips up to meet his thrust. They squirmed in this position with a slow, steady, continuing insertion that thrilled each one in their own way, but together they aroused each other so that there was no other joy to have except the complete pleasure of rapture to each and every fiber of their bodies.

They slept and woke intermittently through the night, reaching for each other to find all the hidden pleasures that a first time discovers. His manliness was firm and well filled with excitement as he pulled her to him in a spoon position. He held her breasts as he slid his firm self from behind into her. She moaned a joyful cry as he penetrated her, and she marveled in the pleasure he was giving her with his body. His breath on her neck added a tingling sensation that brought her straight to another orgasm as he too reached his gratification. Together, they collapsed in thankful joy for each other. There they slept, waking often to find each other's movement further igniting the joy of each other, only to fall back to sleep again in each other's arms.

CHAPTER 10

The morning symphony of birds in the trees outside the bedroom window and the sun streaming through the windows warmed Jen's soul more than usual and beckoned that it was time for the two lovers to wake to face a new day together. Jen quietly got out of bed, leaving Brason snuggled in a sleep she did not want to disturb, as he had a long day ahead and could use the extra sleep. She headed for the kitchen to clear away the dinner dishes and to prepare some perked coffee and set the table for breakfast while she took a shower, getting ready to greet her lover. Her shower seemed especially sensual this morning as the warm water flowed over her satisfied body. Then, as if on cue, Brason was inside the shower with her, and together they felt the warm water flowing over their bodies as one. He soaped her, and she reciprocated his kindness. The touches were not with the passion of the night, but more gentle and precious, loving each other in a more intimate touch Jen had never felt before, and Brason had never offered to anyone before. It was new feelings for both.

"Coffee smells delicious," he said as he exited the guest room, where his luggage had been placed, in a casual outfit for his trip back home. "I dressed for travel because I wanted to leave the horseback ride for another time when I return. Is that okay with you?"

"Of course. You are as handsome this morning as you were the first time I saw you at the cocktail party in the hotel. How long ago was that? Weeks? Months? Years?" He came to her with a hug and a gentle kiss on the cheek.

"It's Sunday, and I usually make French toast with scrambled egg whites and turkey bacon. Is that a menu satisfactory to you? After all, I am just getting to learn about your likes and dislikes."

"It is just what I might make for myself were I cooking. Some hot sauce for my scrambled eggs, okay?"

"Of course, hot sauce. I learned that a while ago from a guy from Georgia."

After breakfast, they walked to the barn to see the horses, and then they walked past the paddock into the apple orchard for a bit, aware that the time was quickly passing and it would soon be time for them to say goodbye to each other until the next time, whenever that might be. They walked holding hands but with intense silence.

"Let's go back, if you don't mind," Brason broke the silence. "I have to make some calls. I generally call my grandmother on Sunday mornings before she goes to church."

"Of course, no problem. Do you go to church on Sunday?"

"Sometimes, but not for the long hours that most of my family does. Do you?"

"Yes, usually I go about 11:00, but not today."

They went back to the house, and he called his grandmother, telling her what a wonderful time he had at the conference and that he had met someone he thought she would like. "Her name is Jenni Noveletti. She is Italian-American and as beautiful as anyone I have ever met—and smart," Jen heard him say. Jen felt warmed by his words because, as she thought about his leaving, she realized they had no plans as to when they would see each other again. That became the difficulty of a long-distance relationship. There are so many loose threads in each other's lives that must be pulled together. He said goodbye to his grandmother, placed the phone in its cradle, and turned to Jen with open arms. She cuddled into them, and they kissed, not goodbye, but simply a kiss that stated that they were good together and that love might see them through the troubled waters of discrimination and fear. Then, he gathered his suitcase and jacket. It was time to get to the American Airlines departure. They discussed keeping in touch as he gave Jen his private telephone extension at his State House Office and his home telephone number. Jen exchanged her numbers with him, too. Both found it sad that the perfect time together was coming to an end, but they were extremely happy to have had the extra time together to learn about each other, what each wanted in the future, and their life goals.

Since it was Sunday, the traffic to the airport was minimal and the ride was quick. Jen decided that she would not park the car and go to the gate with him, though American had an easy parking lot right in front of the departure entrance. It seemed just right to kiss and say "until next time" and not linger. The time was at its end for now.

CHAPTER 11

Monday came as a windy, cold, rainy morning, which made Jen feel dreary and even more dreadful. Everywhere in the house, Jen could feel Brason's presence. She arrived at the office ahead of the crowd to reset her workspace. The box of items the carriers picked up at the hotel was neatly placed on her desk, so it was easy to readjust her environment for the week ahead. Looking at the clock, it read 8:50 a.m. Jen knew Nancy would soon come crashing through the door all a-flutter, having dropped off her baby daughter at her mother's and taken the 6-year-old son to school. Within seconds of her observation, Nancy was at Jen's desk.

"Okay, give me the step-by-step details of how the week went. Did you have a good time? Did you meet anyone exciting? Come on, tell me!" she vociferously begged for her vicarious dose of drama.

"Nancy, it was beyond my expectations. The conference was so exciting for me. I got to work with several committees, taking notes and organizing them for each person in the committee, and the issues were even more important. Each administrative secretary coordinated their committee's work, and I got to put the various works together in a book ready for the printer. I had such—"

"No, no, come on, get to the good part."

"That *is* the good part," Jen replied, knowing full well what she meant. She thought, *"I, of course, will have to censor most of the weekend events; otherwise, the entire State House will know how Attorney General Brason Washington spent his weekend in the home*

"Oh, Jen, you gotta tell me what was exciting, and I'll tell you all about baby diapers and washing clothes. Please make my day."

"Okay, but anything I tell you must be kept in confidence. Promise?"

"Yes, I promise. Now, tell me all the sexy details."

"I didn't go to all the parties like I told you I would because the days were long and very tiring. So, the first few days I did my work and went home for dinner and a good night's rest. The next day was also very busy and intense. I wanted to do a good job; after all, I never know when one of the AGs would offer me a job in his office."

"Did you get an offer?"

"No, but I did get a ride home to my studio by Scott."

"Scott? How'd ya manage that?"

"Well, I think I was being investigated."

"Investigated? For what? What'd ya do?"

"I didn't do anything. The only thing I did was sit and talk with Attorney General Washington, who is the most handsome, mixed-race, gorgeous man you can imagine. He is movie-star quality, bright and intelligent. The Angels of Doom had their eyes on him all night. However, I worked with him in one of the Committees during the week, but never got a chance to talk or anything. I couldn't help but notice how handsome he was, but I did my work and never anything else until he cornered me as I got my drink at the—"

"Cornered you? Where? How? Did you resist?"

"No, silly, I couldn't. I was at the bar, which was set up in the main ballroom of the hotel for our Cocktail Party. As I turned to go back to the group, he stepped in front of me out of nowhere. Gosh, he took my breath away."

"You're in love? Aren't you?"

"No, and I can't fall for anyone now. My father would kill me if I brought home any man, let alone a Black man. OH, MY GOD! Even though Brason is gorgeously handsome and successful, my father would still kill me… at least disown me.

"Brason had gathered a fine group of attorneys who would continue the party for a dinner at a local restaurant. These partygoers invited me to go with them to dinner, but I was just too tired and—"

"Too tired? Are you insane? You can sleep when you're dead."

"No, the next day was Friday, the night of the Formal Dinner. I wanted to be up for that, but I was unsure if I would go because I would have to go alone and sit with the Angels of Doom. You know how uncomfortable that would be for me. Then, the group walked to the outside, where there was a cab waiting. I was going to get a cab to take me to my studio, but as soon as I began to motion for one, Scott, who had been walking behind Mr. Washington and me, said that he would be happy to take me home."

Jen told Nancy all that had transpired, including the call to Scott from Mr. Washington, who asked her to be his dinner partner for the formal dinner when Scott turned the phone over to her.

"Oh my gosh! Oh my gosh… I can't believe this. This is too special. The Attorney General asked you to be his dinner partner? How romantic! The Angels of Doom must have been jealous with envy."

"On that note, we will have to wait. The staff is filing into the office, and life is back to usual for all of us. I will be leaving the office a little earlier today because I have a law exam at 7:00 p.m. and want a few hours to gather my thoughts and review my notes."

After taking Brason to the airport on Sunday, Jen stopped by her parents' for lunch and then went home to study. Fortunately, she has always been able to compartmentalize her mind, especially to study. However, Jen did think of him and wonder if the two days were just that—two days of seclusion where no one knew them or what they were doing. Existence was suspended for them. Jen allowed herself a 3-minute entry back into the moments together and relived the touch of his skin and the beauty of his body, but *she must not linger*. "*I have too much at stake and far too much work to accomplish*," Jen warned herself. "Time to focus."

At her coffee break, Nancy wanted to talk more about the parties and who was there. "What did they wear?" But Jen seldom, if ever, took a coffee break. She worked right through to lunch, often leaving the office for a quiet place to study. Jen knew how anxious Nancy was to hear more about whatever gossip might be juicy enough to chat with others in the office. Most of Nancy's office pals were Civil Service employees, many from other departments of the agency. They had their jobs for life, while those like Jen were held at the will of the present elected official holding the office. Today, Jen actually ended the day at 1:00 p.m. to study at school. By tomorrow, Nancy would have more gossip than Jen could have imagined. She would learn how things were really going tomorrow. Jen was off to take the exam. She would stay at the studio tonight.

"See you tomorrow, Nancy," she called as she raced out of the office and down the hall to the spiral staircase and out the side door, where Joe, the security guard, always welcomed her in the morning and said, "Have a good evening, Little Lady," every night when Jen passed him.

"Will do, Joe. Thanks, you too," she replied as she left the State House, heading for the law class at Suffolk University, where she took classes and met with friends, Jaimie and Sasha, to match notes for the 7:00 p.m. class.

Jaimie was a very bright student, graduating magna cum laude from Colby College in Maine, and Sasha came from Howard University in Washington, D.C. Though Black, Sasha wanted to feel the same acceptance and belonging that the others did. They found a bond upon entry as first-year law students. The three musketeers had managed to stay together through the years.

"Hey, Jen, come sit with us," Jaimie called to their friend from across the dining hall, as Jen picked up a bowl of vegetable soup and headed for her friends.

"Okay, give us the scoop on what went down with the handsome AG," Sasha questioned. "Do you think I should meet him?"

"Forget it, girls. This is one that I think I could actually fall for. He's not only outrageously gorgeous, but he is kind and sweet and—"

"Great in bed?"

"Stop, you guys. Right now, I have nothing to tell except that it was a really nice time we spent together. He hasn't called yet, but he said he would."

"Oh, ya, you know how guys are—they say they'll call, but somehow never do."

"It's okay. I floated past the table where the mean Angels of Doom sat alone, together, all girls. While all I did with great pleasure was walk past them, and as I did, I smiled demurely, holding on to the arm of the Attorney General, and sat at the designated table with my date. What a wonderful feeling."

"Well, I hope he calls." Jaimie tuned in. "Now, let's look at notes to be certain we have everything the professor said would be on the test."

The next several hours, Jen and her friends spent going over each other's notes. Then they put it all aside for a little fun and relaxation in the sports room, a light dinner at 5:30 p.m., and then to focus on the test. Expectations were that they would all pass.

Sleeping at the studio was a sleepless effort, as Jen could only think that she had not heard from Brason. She had neither a personal phone nor any other phone at the studio. She knew he must have been very busy, having been out of the office for the entire week of the conference. Sleep finally came from sheer exhaustion of the energy exerted over the week.

Tuesday passed quickly, and Nancy informed Jen that some of the girls were talking about the 'handsome guy Jen was seen with,' but others had negative comments: 'How can she go with a black guy? A mixed relationship will only bring trouble along the way.' There were many more derogative remarks, too.

"Oh, Nancy, you know I have no prejudices against people of color, religion, or various cultures. I love everybody. I find goodness in everything, don't I?"

"Yes, but you are sometimes so 'Pollyanna-ish' that you seem to live in another world."

"Yah, maybe I do, but I love it in my tower. You know, like Rapunzel, waiting for her Prince Charming to come save her."

"Yah, but you're going to have a whole lot of trouble in this community, in these troubled days, with your father and a whole lot of people. Little girl, you're heading for big trouble."

"Oh, Nancy, your gloom and doom are so depressing. So, stop it. Okay?"

"Okay, Jen, but I care for you, and I'm afraid for you. I'm here to talk, if you wish. Okay?"

"Okay!"

Jen left that conversation for another time, but the thought that the staff was talking about Brason in a negative way, not knowing what a wonderful man he was, bothered Jen immensely. These were only the people with whom she worked. How would her family take to her serious relationship with a Black man, and what would it do to their relationship?

On her way home, Jen stopped by her long-time girlfriend's house, as she often did. Alice and her husband were watching the news. It showed a riot where white police were being physically combative with a group of Black peaceful protesters, using clubs and water sprays to hold them back. Tensions had been growing, and peaceful demonstrations had turned into massacres. Jen mentioned with great concern how terrible it was and that she felt so bad for the Blacks and the conditions that they were in. Suddenly, Alice's husband, who never talked much to Jen, went on a rampage, yelling that Jen was "a nigga luva." Jen was astonished. She tried to defend her feelings, but to no avail. All he did was scream, "You're a nigga luva; a nigga lover!" He was not just angry; he was killer-angry. Jen apologized. Alice kissed Jen goodbye, and Jen turned to leave straight away, feeling the pain of how someone Black might feel in such a circumstance.

"I must go. I'm so sorry."

The week passed quickly with work, school, and finally TGIF Friday came. Jen believed that on Friday, she should be on her way home by 3:00 p.m., no matter where she worked. So, with a quick "Have a good weekend!" to everyone, Jen told Nancy she was going to stop at her mom's before going home. She left the office and headed out. Brason had not called during the week. Jen was too upset and too busy to call him. Furthermore, girls were not supposed to call boys in those days. It was improper behavior for a young woman. Traffic had not yet begun to build on the way home, so the ride was pleasant as Jen left the city bustle and drove toward the place she called "the country." Mom and Dad lived only a few miles from Jen's home, but in the richer part of town.

CHAPTER 12

"Hi, Mom," Jen greeted her as she came bursting into the kitchen where her mom was preparing dinner.

"Hi, Jen. I got a call from some guy who says the secretary at your office gave him this number. Who is it—a new guy?"

"Well, kinda. I've been waiting for him to call all week. Wouldn't you know that the day I leave early, he calls?"

"Who is he? Where did you meet him?" her mom asked in her mother-must-know-all voice.

"Where's Dad?"

"He is outside checking his tomato plants. They are doing quite nicely. And now back to this new guy."

"Mom, he is absolutely the most handsome man I've ever met. He is intelligent, he is successful, he is kind, he is sweet, and I've only known him for one week. But at the beginning of last week, he was for me nothing but another Attorney General in the committee meetings, just a brilliant mind to work with and enjoy my position. Then he cornered me at the cocktail party, and we hit it off so well that he asked me to be his dinner partner at the formal night. I accepted, and we had another great time together at the dinner, where we danced until we were the only ones left."

"Did you sleep with him?" her mom asked in her usual accusing way.

"Mom, please. I did go back to his hotel suite, and we both fell asleep, but did nothing but sleep. The next day, I promised I would take him on a tour of the ride of Paul Revere and to the Battle of Lexington and Concord. Even then, we had a wonderful time together. I invited him to stay for dinner and the night, so he canceled his flight until Sunday, and we had a 'Get to know you' evening. I even sang for him." Jen told her mom about what she served for dinner and how it all went so well, but said nothing else.

"He sounds dreamy. He left his number for you to call him. Are you going to see him again?"

"Well, I hope so, but distance is the trouble, and both of us are very busy people."

"Hi, Dad," she said as he entered the kitchen, admiring a couple of tomatoes for lunch.

"Jen, are you staying for supper?" her dad asked.

"I've made your favorite eggplant dish," her mom stated.

"No, I must get home. I have a lot of study this weekend, and I still have to unpack things from last week. Just too much to do, but I'll come by and pick you and Grandpa up for Mass. As a matter of fact, where is Grandpa?"

"He's taking a nap on the patio," her dad interjected.

"Okay, I just stopped by for a moment. Gotta get home."

With that, Jen kissed everyone, but did not go out to the patio to kiss her grandpa. He was clever and would see right through her. He would begin to ask questions about this new guy who called. Grandpa was always right to the point without holding back on anything he wanted to know.

"As things progress, I will certainly tell him and ask Grandpa for his thoughts and what he thinks. I will listen to his wise evaluation of the situation. But for now, I must begin to make some decisions on my own. It is time for me to grow up," she thought.

CHAPTER 13

Jen enjoyed the ride home past well-manicured lawns and flowering trees to her own little country estate. It was a lovely spring day with flowers blooming all over the city. Now, as she approached her sweet little house, the trees and the welcoming flowers blossomed and filled her world with the effervescence of all the beauty displayed in the landscape. Jen was happy with her life. She treasured her family's love. Jen picked up the mail and entered the empty house. She released the alarm system and put away the stuff for the weekend's study. She then went to the fridge and took a small bottle of Pinot, poured it, and took the number Brason had left with Mom for her to call. Jen took a sip of wine and sat down to make the call.

The phone rang a few times, and then Brason's voice came on with the excitement and energy only he exuded. "Hello, Brason here!"

"Hi, Brason, this is Jenni. You do remember me, don't you?"

"Oh, Jen, it seems like a lifetime since we've been together. I've missed you terribly."

"I've missed you, too. I left work early today. I was so tired. It has been a very stressful week with a lot of gossip about us—the Black guy Jen was with, and more."

"I wouldn't worry about that. They are just jealous because I had the most beautiful girl in the State House as my dinner partner."

"Oh, Brason, you are really sweet, but I think a little unrealistic."

"Okay, I miss you, so let's look at our calendars and see what we can do to be together again. I have to be in New York City, possibly next month. Would you be able to meet me there? I arrive on the third Tuesday of the month and will stay until Sunday morning."

"Oh, that would be wonderful, but I have finals that week with a group, and I have to study for the sample state exam on Saturday. There is no way that I would be able to carve out time then. I could only have maybe Sunday, if my parents don't have something going on Sunday."

"Well, just fly down for the night, and we'll go to dinner and have a relaxing evening together. Does it sound good?"

"Brason, I want to see you, but I'm not certain that I can do it. I will let you know as soon as I can."

"I guess this is what will happen with a long-distance relationship. We will adjust to whatever it is that we must. Let's see how it all works out. What are you doing this weekend?"

"Not much—just cleaning the house a little and studying a lot. I'm doing really well in my work, and I have been interviewing with some civil rights judges for a position. Also, a representative from the government came to school to offer a year's opportunity to work in Prague or at the United Nations on a study program of human rights. I don't know where it will take me, but it's a beginning and a challenge."

"Remember, you can come work for me on my campaign."

"Yes. Thank you, but there are so many things to consider for my career."

"Okay, I won't smother you. I just miss you so much. I've told my grandma about you, and she is eager to meet you. Have you told your mother about me?"

"Yes, in a general manner. I told her how handsome, intelligent, and successful you are."

"Did you tell her that I am not white?"

"No, I didn't get that far. I thought I would wait until I was certain that we would be able to make it together. I hope you are okay with that?"

"Certainly, but the sooner we tell them, the easier it will be. We must not wait too long."

"Okay, I will tell them the next time we are together. What are you doing this weekend?"

"I'm knocking on doors and talking to people so they know what I'm all about and that they need me as the governor of their state."

"They will be so fortunate to have you as their Governor. I will say a little prayer for you each day as you travel on the campaign trail. Hatred is surfacing with violence. It frightens me."

"Yes, but we cannot bury our heads in the sand or run from what is the truth. We cannot let bigots take over our lives. We will overcome with peaceful demonstrations."

"Please be careful. Get a bodyguard for your safety, please. Martin Luther King seems to be making some real excitement. He instills hope in the hearts of those of us who believe in civil rights at a cost beyond acceptance. I am afraid for us. I'm becoming afraid for all of us, for this country, and for our democracy. There is such evil in the world, run by those wanting to destroy our constitutional culture."

"Jen, please, you must be strong if we expect this to work. I know; I love you, and I know that we will have a beautiful life together, and our children will be geniuses and absolute knockouts. Please, we will rise above all the slime of the time. One day, as King said in his 'I Have a Dream' speech during the March on Washington on August 28, 1963… that little children will one day live in a nation where they will not be judged by the color of their skin but by the content of their character. Well, Jen, I, too, have that same dream for you and me and the children we will have. Don't be frightened. I will be your strength. We will flourish. Now, wipe your eyes. I can hear your sniffles. Tell me you will come to New York. We will have a quiet, romantic dinner in an out-of-the-way French restaurant I know called Pierre's, very near where I am staying at the Theresa Hotel, known as the Waldorf of Harlem. Black folk haven't made it to the Oak Room at the Plaza yet, but one day we will stay there in a suite overlooking the park. I promise."

"Darling, I will think about this. I will let you know if that is doable for me to meet you. Falling in love with you was not one of the things I had on my list of things to accomplish this year. As I get to know you, I love you more. Nonetheless, we have a long way to go. I will call you next week. Be careful and think of me."

"I think of you all the time. I replay our time together, and I love the 'bubble we lived in' when we were together. It was wonderful. No one knew we existed. I will send you a ticket when you decide to come."

"Love you. Until next week, I'll be thinking of you every day."

"Me too. I love you."

CHAPTER 14

Jen and Brason promised to call each other whenever they had some free time. However, free time for the likes of Brason meant no time for anything more than six hours' sleep, if he could manage it. On the other hand, Jen required at least seven to eight hours' sleep due to the pressures of her workday. As a child, Jen suffered from a heart murmur, for which she had no visible disabilities, but it was to be watched. She had an unusually high energy level, but as soon as she hit the pillow, she was in dreamland.

"I do not have the energy that Brason has, which is far beyond mine," Jen thought as she fell off to sleep.

"I promise to call before I go to sleep," Jen said, meaning it but knowing it would not be easy.

"I will try to do the same," Brason responded, equally knowing how difficult it would be.

With both promising to do their very best, they sent a kiss through the phone, said good night to each other, and reluctantly each hung up the phone.

"It is amazing how a busy person is always able to squeeze things into a busy schedule, except when they are not certain what to do or say."

The next three weeks were arduous and exhausting. Jen was working, studying, testing, and the worst distraction, waiting to hear from Brason. Then they endured the frustration of calling each other when one or the other was not available. All the stress was beginning to show on Jen's face.

Mother had warned, "You are looking thinner."

While Nancy warned, "Where's that joyful Jen? I have not seen that happy, smiling, pretty face in weeks."

"What's up, girl?" Nancy asked one Friday before leaving for the weekend. "I'm worried about you."

"Oh, Nancy, it's been only two months since I met Brason, but it feels more like two years. I have not been able to study with undivided attention. All the questions about us and our needs require answers, and it's wearing me down. All of it fills my head and makes me dizzy. I have not told my parents that Brason is Black. I've only told my mother how wonderful he is. Whenever I bring up the subject in an attempt to discuss the civil rights movement or the massacres of Blacks to get into the heart of it all, hoping to lead to the mention of Brason, they change the subject by saying that they understand the problems of the Blacks, but it doesn't affect us, and it certainly doesn't affect anything I'm doing. 'Let's not discuss it. You know how your father gets upset discussing politics,' is Mom's only comment."

"They are just trying to keep the bad things away from you. They know how sweet you are, and you see nothing but "good" in all things. However, we are living in a world that has hate, prejudice, and evil in it. Your parents are simply trying to protect you, just as I am, from the hurts of the day."

"Nancy, I don't think I can be strong enough to combat all the evil that is directed at people who are of a different color or at those who associate with them. I watch whites get beaten up by the police in peaceful demonstrations. It upsets me so."

"You have so much potential in your future, why add what could be a disastrous result? You should only hear the evil, distasteful remarks being made by some of our co-workers about what your parents should do to save you?"

"Save me? What kind of remarks, Nancy?"

"One jerk said that if he were your father, he would have you committed to an asylum for your own protection."

"Come on, Nancy, a father cannot commit a perfectly sane person to an asylum, can he?"

"According to some, this was the only way to stop interracial unions from occurring, and some families took that approach."

"My father would never do that to me!"

"I would hope not, but it can be done, and it would be legal."

"Oh, my heavens, I can't believe that I am in this situation."

"Jen, you have that really nice attorney coming after you. He shows up just to sit and have lunch with you. He is a State Representative and a successful real estate attorney. Why not go after him? I'm certain your parents would love him."

"Yes, that's Robert. He is Italian, handsome, and educated, and his family is one of the major distributors of food in our state. He's a great catch."

"What are your plans for this weekend? We're going to Falmouth. Would you like to come?"

"I'd love to bu—"

"Ya, BUT you have to stay home waiting for a call from Mr. Wonderful, right?"

"No! On Saturday night, my parents are having Robert and his parents at the Country Club for dinner. It should be really fun, and I am looking forward to relaxing, dancing with my father, and enjoying my family and friends. No thoughts of Brason, if I can manage it."

"Good thinking! You have so much life filled with joy and success ahead; I'd hate to see you destroy it for Mr. Brason."

"Thank you, Nancy. I know you have my interests as your top priority."

"Well, my pet, I'm happy that you will be with your family this weekend. Have a super time, and look at Robert with a keen eye to your future."

Jen said goodbye to Nancy and hoped she would have a super fabulous weekend on the Cape with her family.

CHAPTER 15

It was 5:00 p.m., Friday. Time to meet the gang for a drink at the Rusty Scupper, primarily a singles bar, for a few laughs and an early night at home. This was Jen's one night when she could let down her guard and just enjoy the banter of attorneys, stockbrokers, salespersons, and secretaries together after a long week of solving issues. Finally, it was time to just tease each other with their sexuality and see who would go home with whom. It was fun, it was the '60s, and yes, Jen had her eye on the electrical engineer who was tall, dark, and quite handsome, but since he had come to the Scupper with a girl Jen knew, he was off-limits. They always managed to talk for a while as Jen stopped around to chat with other friends. It was Jen's "reeelaaaxation" time. She had fun but often went home alone. She was geographically undesirable.

Jen left the Scupper and arrived home at about 10:30 p.m. The phone was ringing as she rushed into the house, turned off the alarm, and picked up the phone.

"Hello."

"Hello, my love, it's been difficult to reach you. I've called intermittently throughout the week, but with little result. What have you been doing?"

"Oh, my darling, I have been thinking of you and waiting to hear from you. I, too, have called you intermittently but have been unsuccessful in reaching you. How are you?"

"I'm fine. Just working very hard and doing all the footwork that is necessary to set up campaign headquarters in various cities in the States. Have you reconsidered coming to New York this weekend?"

"Yes, well, no… no, I cannot come."

"I will send you the ticket," he said, pushing to get his way.

"No, I can't. My folks are having a small party at the Club, and I must go with them."

"Well, it's a perfect time for me to meet them. It's been almost two months. So, I will come to your party. How's that sound?"

"Oh, no, Brason, that is not possible. I have not even told my parents about you, except to tell my mom that we met and you are wonderful. Unfortunately, my parents would not be ready to see you under these circumstances."

"This is a little uncomfortable for me. When do you think you will be able to tell them about us?"

"Soon. I promise."

"The Fourth of July is coming next month, and you are invited to come to our family's annual celebration. It has been going on every year since my granddad rebuilt his business in Black Wall Street. All my uncles, aunts, cousins, and childhood friends will be there, and it would be a perfect time for me to introduce you as my fiancée."

"Brason, you are so wonderful, I don't know how I could refuse such a wonderful invitation, but I think it is much too soon for us to become engaged. It is only spring, and I have graduation and study for the Bar. I was planning to take it in July or February. It is all too much, all at once. I thought we might just take time during this next year to learn how we manage together. I cannot rush. I love you, but I still can't rush."

"Okay, I understand. I know how frightened you are of the world, and I don't want to contribute to that discomfort. I see things so clearly, and the mixed race does not bother me because I see us in our little bubble where no one can harm us."

"Who is being naive now, Mr. Washington? I am hearing stories that make me very uncomfortable."

"Okay, let's put those all aside, and I will come to Boston. I must see you so we can hold on to the threads that have knitted us together."

"That would be fantastic, bu—"

"No buts about it. I will arrive at 10:30 a.m., Saturday. We will spend the day together, then you will go out to dinner with your family, and after that, you will come home. I'd like to go to Boston to a really super jazz bar. I'm not certain who is performing, but there are some people I want to meet. It will be fun. Come on, baby. Please."

"Brason, I don't think it will work. My parents have this dinner party that I am expected to attend."

"We can have the day together; you can attend their dinner party and then come home so we can be together until Sunday, when I must get back home to organize and fly out on Monday for campaign stops."

"That seems doable—but it's a lot of pressure on me to act relaxed and happy when I am stressed and unhappy, not being with you."

"Think about it and just say yes."

After a long pause: "Okay, then, yes, Brason, come to Boston. I can hardly wait to see you. It seems that is all that matters to me."

"Okay, then, I will rent a car, and if all schedules are on time, I will be at your house on Saturday at about 10:30 a.m. See you then."

"Yes, my love, I'll see you."

Jen went into the living room and sat looking out the picture window onto the flowers of spring and cried. She was confused about her life, but not about what she felt for Brason. Was it possible to love someone so much yet not be able to fulfill a life with this person because of so many obstacles that could almost NEVER be changed? Jen cried most of that night as she fell asleep on the sofa, waking the next day with a slight pain in her back from the uncomfortable position in which she slept.

"I don't think you are doing very well," she cajoled her image in the reflection she saw in the large mirror she often sang before in her candlelit living room.

Jen still had two weeks to dissuade Mom from changing the dinner party to the following week, allowing her to have the full weekend with Brason. Dad was unrelenting, for it seemed that something special was happening at the club on that date. The date was set, and that was it.

"Dad was as stubborn as Brason. What a pair to have to deal with," Jen thought. *"Well, I guess I have no choice but to let it all play out as it should."*

Jen then set about doing the chores she had listed on her "Things to do!"

1. Laundry

2. Grocery shopping

3. Some weeding in the flower patches

4. Lots of study

It was the way she spent most of her weekends. Now, it was with a pressure she had never experienced before.

The two weeks went flashing by with research tasks at work, studying, testing, keeping Mom from asking questions about Brason, and Mom telling Jen the grand qualities of Robert, who would be joining them for dinner at the Country Club next Saturday.

Nancy spent those weeks watching over Jen like a mother hen, making certain she had proper food to eat as she brought Jen a taste of the dinner from the night before. Jen was very grateful for her concern, but it seemed she now had two mothers. One was difficult to handle, but two were overwhelming.

"Be certain to take some time to actually eat something today. You are beginning to look like an ad from one of the world hunger organizations."

"Nancy, I am being pressured to tell my parents that Brason is a Black man. I am having a great deal of trouble because my dad will go through the roof. He is, after all, somewhat of a bigot."

"Well, don't tell them right now. Wait until you have spent a bit more time with Brason. After all, a couple of months doesn't allow you to know him very well. It will be great for you to accept the invitation to the family's Fourth of July event. You will have an opportunity to see how he reacts to his family. You will be able to see how they interact with you. If it doesn't feel right, then you can look at what you will face with the world if you become Mrs. Washington."

"I'm so glad that I have you in my life. You pull away the weeds so I can see the plants and their roots. I want this to grow into a strong, loving relationship. I feel we have it when we are in our little 'bubble,' but I'm so weak when it comes to standing up and declaring my intentions. I seem unable to hold up my end of this mixed relationship. I am truly frightened by the outside world; not our loving each other, but the hate outside our bubble."

"Jen, some people have the ability to tackle unimaginable consequences in their lives, and others just cannot. Relax and think only of where you are going in your career and your life. You have a great number of issues to consider, including those of your unborn children and how they will manage in a world where they will be neither Black nor white. What kind of life will they experience? How will you guide them? Yes, Jen, you have a lot on your list of decisions to be made. Just relax and let life lead you. Then see what happens!"

"Yikes, look at the time. I gotta go, gotta work…" Jen said as she went back to her desk and began working on a desegregation brief.

Every day in the Department of the Attorney General was hectic, as each division had so much work to accomplish. Jen was doing so well both in school and in the department. She was happy with everything, except the issue with Brason. She had a great many chores to finish before Brason came to town. The week went rather slowly. Brason and Jen had not spoken since last week, when he told her he would come to Boston if she could not make it to New York City. He would not listen to her pleading with him to wait until another date that might be more convenient. Jen was beginning to see that Brason usually got what he wanted. He was able to manipulate anything into his favor. At least that is what Jen had been able to observe. While she, on the other hand, tended to go with the flow, sometimes ending up in a situation she had never quite thought out completely. Here she was in this situation, determined to handle it however it materialized.

When they finally reached each other during the following week, Jen had managed to organize and re-evaluate the relationship so she would be ready for whatever Brason and the relationship produced. If he wanted to come to her house early on Saturday and wait while she had dinner with her parents and their friends, then return home as early as possible to go out with him and spend the rest of the weekend together, then that was what would happen.

"When I get home, I will call Brason to tell him my decision," she thought.

"Hi, Brason. I am so happy to reach you. What's all that rowdy, female, boisterous yelling I hear?"

"Just a few organizers, excited about the poll figures. They are really good."

"Okay, just as long as you are not in harm's way. I know how attractive candidates are to young, impressionable volunteers. Now, here is what I've been thinking. I thought seriously about your plan to come to Boston on Saturday. I think, if that is what you want to do, then let's do it. I will trust in your determination and logical thinking to make it all happen. I will see you at my house on Saturday, at about 10:30 a.m. in the morning. Until then, just know that I have missed you every minute of each and every day. You left a joy within me that I cannot explain. I can hardly wait to see and be with you again. Hurry back, my love."

"I love you, Jen. I will be beside you as soon as I possibly can."

"I am sending you a thousand kisses until I am able to kiss you with all the love I know I have inside me for you. Hold all those delicious thoughts, hug your pillow, and I will be with you very soon," he said.

They said goodbye to each other and hung up the phone.

Finally, Friday came, and although Jen's usual decision was to go to the Scupper and hang out after work, today she decided to go home directly. However, she had an interesting call for lunch. It was the tall, dark, handsome engineer whose name was Ed, asking if she was free for lunch.

"I'd love to, but can't. Incidentally, what about the girl I see you with?"

"Oh, ya, Jen, I only saw her a few times at the Scupper, but there is nothing much between us. Come to lunch, and we will talk all about it, okay?"

"Can't do it today, but maybe next week."

"Fine. I hope you have a nice weekend. I will call you at the beginning of the week. Until then…"

"See you soon."

(At lunch with Nancy the next week.)

"My life is full, and I have several very good prospects in my life. Brason is not 'the only fish in my fish tank.'"

"At least the few men you date are well educated and considered a 'good catch' by any mother's standards."

"Also, Nancy, I don't tell my parents about every guy I date. I'm certain there would be some they definitely would not like my dating. I've put all that out of my mind and concentrated on the moment. I guess that is not what I have been doing very well lately…

concentrating on the moment. With so many variables on my mind, it has become difficult."

It would have been a delightful lunch, except her reaction to Ed's invitation to lunch had distressed her. Somehow, the fact that she even considered accepting the invitation to lunch with Ed made Jen realize that Brason was such a small part of her world. It was just months ago that they met.

"That's hardly enough time to determine that you are in love," she thought. *"I still don't have a proper understanding of LOVE. I'm too busy preparing for my future as a civil rights attorney."*

It was Friday. Jen decided she would go home directly after work.

"No Scupper tonight. My week has been filled with too much excitement. I need my home in the country; the apple orchard, the horses in the barn, my environment for balance. I need to sleep peacefully, quietly, and soundly in my comfortable bed."

A sound sleep had not happened in weeks for Jen. She was ready for it tonight.

CHAPTER 16

The drive back to the country was exhilarating and refreshing. Upon arriving home, the flowering tree in the front of the house was in bloom. It pleased Jen to her soul. The lawn had been mowed, and everything looked lovely and ready for the incredible weekend ahead. Jen went directly to her bedroom, removed her business suit, and got into comfortable jeans. She strolled out to the barn to see what was happening there. It appeared the horses had been fed and groomed and were happy. The day was cool while the sun was warm. Trees and flowers were in bloom everywhere. Everything was in a happy mode as Jen strolled back to the house to make a light dinner, watch some TV, play some piano, and read before falling asleep.

Saturday morning was a beautiful, sunny day with no humidity and birds cheerily chanting in the trees just outside her bedroom window.

(Phone rings. Jen answers it, knowing it's her mom.)

"Good morning, Mom. Yes, it's a gorgeous day. Well, no, I won't be coming by this morning. I have errands to do and some grocery shopping, or I won't have any food for next week. I have some studying and house cleaning to do, or the Dept. of Health will close me down. No, Mom, no… I will drive my car and meet everyone at the Club at 5:30 p.m. No. No."

Jen was not happy with the way the call ended since the entire day had to go according to the Brason plan. Brason called about 10 a.m. to say that the plane had landed at Logan and he would be at her house within the hour. Jen had enough time to get to the supermarket for her weekly groceries. She returned home to see a car in the driveway and the handsome, extraordinary man of her heart leaning on the car, holding a bunch of flowers.

"I wanted to get home before you, but what a joy to see you sitting waiting for me. I love you so," she said as she parked her car next to his and exited hers. They moved anxiously toward each other for their first kiss in months.

"Oh, my love, I have missed you with all my heart," Brason whispered in her ear.

They hugged. Then they began to empty Jen's automobile of groceries and his two suitcases. At some point in this process, Mrs. Whitney, the next-door neighbor, came out for her mail. She waved to Jen. "How are things going? Looks like you have company for the weekend! Have a good day," she said as she went back inside.

"Oh, my goodness, she will be watching through the bedroom curtains all weekend."

"Let's not pay any attention to Mrs. Whitney. She probably eats only white bread and has a disdainful attitude toward Blacks mixing with whites, so let's go inside and shut out the rest of the world," he said as they took in the last items in the cars.

When they closed the doors behind them, Jen and Brason melted into the "bubble" they had found the first night they spent in this home, only a few short times ago.

"You must be tired from an entire week of meetings in New York?"

"Yes, but I am so happy to be here with you, and I am looking forward to the ride in the orchard, if that is still on the events list?"

"As long as the kid isn't off riding somewhere with his friend."

This was the conversation that walked them down the hall to Jen's bedroom. Jen had given this love part of their relationship much thought, but those thoughts still were not strong enough to blot out all the negative fears she had been harboring, nor the atrocious scenes she had been seeing on TV of police brutality against Blacks, Browns, and white sympathizers in what should have been peaceful demonstrations. She knew her father was seeing these newsreels too, if and when he watched his news. Jen feared her dad, but she also loved him. Her family was part of her life, and their unhappiness, should she choose this Black man, was what was gnawing at her heart. But she put it out of her mind as Brason began to lift the T-shirt over her head as they reached the bedroom. They climbed up onto the bed. As Jen lay back on the pillow, Brason just sat looking admiringly at Jen.

"I want to be certain that what I saw the first night with you is still the same thing I see today in the light."

"It's still me. That girl you invited to be your dinner partner for the formal dinner during the Conference a few months ago… or has it been years ago?" Their unified laugh relaxed into a sweet, passionate kiss that began the entire stream of morning lovemaking. Their lovemaking did not end until they had missed lunch, leaving them famished but with no desire to leave the confines of their love trap. Plus, it would soon be time for Jen to think about getting ready for the real evening's event—dinner at the Country Club.

"Have I told you that I love you, Jen? I really do. I'm so glad that we have this time to balance all the negatives with the positives on both sides. This weekend will be a really good opportunity to test our being together in public, because I have some people to meet while I'm here, and I would like you to be with me."

"It all seems much too soon for me, but I am with you as you wish. I'm going to prepare a small dish of sushi with fruit and cheese for a snack."

"No, please don't bother. I'll just go downtown, look around, and stop in a little coffee shop for something while you're gone. I like doing that, especially where no one knows me."

"Okay, then, I'm going to take a shower. You can watch TV, listen to music, or do whatever you wish. I must get ready. I cannot be late. If I am late, then I cannot excuse myself early to get back here to be with you," Jen said, kissing him lightly on the cheek as she started for her shower.

With the next hours all comfortably arranged and each accomplishing their individual duties, Brason sat on the bed, perusing the backyard out the window. It was truly a lovely piece of property, well-maintained and a credit to this wonderful girl.

"I must ask her how she managed all she has at such an early age," he thought.

He continued to look around the room and noticed that the clothes in her closet were neatly organized. He walked to the kitchen to make a pot of coffee. Everything there was orderly, organized, and clean as well.

"Why, this girl is a prize! She will keep a clean house, not that she will have to do it herself, but it's good to know that she can if necessary."

Brason was very pleased that he was falling in love with this magnificent young woman, who would someday be a magnificent wife.

"She is wonderful," floated through his mind as he took his black coffee into the living room, put on some music, and settled into the very spot where Jen often sat, looking out the window for answers to her questions of life. Brason sat and looked out the same window, listening to the music and hearing Jen prepare for her dinner date with her parents. He would spend this time feeling the environment in which his love lives.

"I'm ready," she said as she emerged from her dressing area, fully dressed in a lovely royal blue sailor-style cocktail dress with brass buttons, looking glamorous, sleek, and gorgeous in Brason's eyes, and certainly in every eye that would look at her tonight.

"I'm lost for words to describe what I see. You are the most beautiful female I've ever seen. Oh, how I wish I were going with you to the Club for dinner."

"Yes, I wish the same. Don't worry, it will happen before you know it. But it is 5:00 now, and I will be on time for Dad, who has probably been at the Club checking to be certain everything is as he ordered it. God love him, he is a tiger... he is tough!"

"Darling, you look fantastic. Enjoy the early part of this night, but come home as soon as possible. We will catch the midnight show at the Jazz Club in Boston if you do. I'll make all the arrangements."

"Brason, here is a key to the house. If you go downtown, you will not have to set the alarm. I think it will be all right. Daytime is not so bad, just be careful. This is primarily a white town now. The Billerica Indians or Shawshin Indians founded the town in the 1630s. It's also known as the 'Yankee Doodle Town,' where the song was written after a man from here was tarred and feathered by the British. So please, let's not get tarred and feathered. Though I don't think they still do that anymore."

"Don't worry, this is not the Deep South. No one will bother me."

"Come here and give me a kiss to hold me over till I get back to you."

Brason obediently left the comfort of the sofa and the beauty of the front yard to capture the kiss Jen offered. They held it together for a few moments, seeming to recall the time together earlier.

"Be charming. Come home early."

"I'll be back as soon as possible. Luv ya…" she said as she left the house, and he waved a kiss at the front door.

CHAPTER 17

Dad was waiting at the valet when Jen arrived at the Country Club, which looked extraordinary with lovely spring flowers overwhelming the entrance. It was like driving into a fairyland. There were times, like this very moment, when Jen thanked the heavens for the benefits she had been given in her life. She was living the perfect life for any person.

"Hi, Dad," she greeted warmly as she exited the automobile, grabbing for his hand as her left leg peeked out of the slit in her dress and lifted her to a standing position.

"Darling, you look beautiful tonight. Come, Mom, and the Salernos are waiting for you."

Dad had a table just off the dance floor, which is where he always sat. He loved to dance, and this was where it was best for him. Dad always managed to get what he wanted. After all the greetings and kisses—first on the right cheek, then on the left—we all sat down. The waitress asked, and we all ordered drinks from the bar. The evening began. The food was always a satisfaction to the palate of anyone, even the most discriminating food reporter. The Club had triple-A ratings, or whatever those ratings are. People loved joining the Club, if only for the social programs. However, the golf course was one of the best in the country.

"My beautiful daughter, may I have this dance?" He extended his hand to her and apologized to the guests at the table. "We will be just a short dance… It's a waltz."

It was a lovely waltz, and, as usual when Jen and her father got on the dance floor, people moved to the sides to watch; those still seated in their seats stopped eating and drinking to watch the two incredibly synchronized dancers glide over the ballroom dance floor, covering every inch of the floor in elegant movements.

"You are my world, dear Jen. You are the very best thing that has ever happened to me in my life. You fill my world with your love, your intelligence, and your beauty. You have a life of happiness and success before you. I will help in any way that I can. You have my emotional and financial support in your law career. Go for it. Also, I think Robert's family really likes you. As for Robert, what do you think?"

"Dad, please, can we just enjoy the dance and the Salernos without applying future scenarios to our being together? Let it be," she murmured as they continued their execution of the waltz.

(The waltz ended, and Jen and her dad returned to the table)

"I'm a bit nervous to ask you for a dance," Robert directed the comment to Jen. "You and your dad are so professional. You might just want to catch your breath first?"

"Yes, that would be nice."

The food was served, so everyone sat and spoke in quiet tones about business. Jen's dad owned a partnership in the meat manufacturing business, and Robert Sr. owned a produce, fruit, and vegetable company. Joining these two Italian families was the dream of a lifetime for both parents. The conversation was pleasant and interesting, but Jen was not fully focused on the conversation, as her attention was also on the clock. It was 10:00 p.m., and she was anxious to get home to Brason. She would have to leave soon, or she and Brason would never make it into town for the midnight jazz, so when Mrs. Salerno suddenly said she was very tired, it was time to make a gracious exit. It was time for Robert Jr. to drive them home because they were all going out in their 65-ft. cruiser on Sunday. Mom and Dad were going with them.

"Would you like to join us, Jen?" Robert Jr. asked.

"Oh, Robert, I'd love to, but this weekend is not good for me, so sorry. Maybe we could set another time?"

"Of course. It was great spending this time with you and your parents. I know you have a great deal of studying, and the last year of law school is only slightly more terrifying than facing the state exam. Don't worry; you will sail right through it all. Call me if you need any help in preparing. I've been through it so that I can help."

"Thank you, Robert. I will call you at some point. Have fun on the water tomorrow. It is guaranteed to be a great day by the weather report."

"Be careful driving home, Jen. Incidentally, you looked absolutely beautiful and professional on the dance floor with your dad. It is obvious that you are the apple of his eye and the light in his heart. He is so very proud of you in every way."

"Thank you again. Yes, I will be careful driving home. I love my dad with all my heart and soul. It's very difficult to disagree with him. I'll see you soon."

"Okay, that's fine," he said as he helped her into her orange Karmann Ghia convertible.

Dad did not understand that Robert Jr. and Jen had been friends since elementary school. They admired and respected each other, but

Robert was a friend and not a 'boyfriend.' However, he could be, but they hadn't even been on a 'date.' They hung out with lots of friends and often went to the same parties, but not together like on a 'date.'

Jen drove back to her house, but as she drove down the street and neared her home, she saw a police car with its lights blinking in the dark night of the countryside.

"What the fuck is this?" Jen slowed down at the direction of the police.

"Sorry, lady, what's your reason for coming down this street?"

"I live in that house. What's going on?"

"It appears that a black man was seen trying to get into your house, and a passing neighbor called the police on a break and enter. We just got here this moment."

"No problem, officer. I have an out-of-town visitor who just happens to be Black. Was it the lady across the street who called?"

"No, I think it was a lady a few doors down on the other side of your house. She was driving by. She said she knew you lived alone and that your car was not out front. When she saw the Black man get out of his car and struggle with the key at the door, she thought he was breaking into the house. Since we don't see many, or practically any, Black folks in this neighborhood, she got startled and called the police."

At that moment, Brason came out the door, moving toward the police and her.

"Officer, I am Attorney General Brason Washington. I am visiting my friend Jen for the weekend. Here are my credentials. Maybe we can resolve this so we can continue with our weekend."

"Yes, of course. Thank you," the officer replied, scrutinizing his documents. "And have a pleasant evening, sir." The police car left; Jen and Brason went into the house.

"Do you suppose I can't leave you for a minute that you won't stir up trouble?" Jen playfully reprimanded him.

"I never stir up trouble," he teased as they faced each other for a kiss. "Now, let's get goin', or we'll never get there on time."

"Maybe we should have asked for a police escort to downtown," Jen jested.

"I don't think so."

Brason was already dressed and ready to go, just as Jen was ready in her lovely cocktail attire. Both were ready for a night on the town, but not before the phone rang. While lifting the phone off the cradle, Jen acknowledged in sign to Brason: *It's only my mother*. "Yes, Mom, I got home all right. No problems. Talk to you tomorrow, and don't call me early. I am not going to Mass tomorrow. Okay! Good night, we all had a super time. Sleep well; me too."

"Does she do that often?"

"Since I have moved here, she has called the police twice because she is worried someone might have broken into the house and held me captive. God bless my mother, but she has placed fear of everything in my life. I'm struggling to stay ahead of her fears, as I often do things that I am frightened of simply to face those fears. It is terribly uncomfortable."

"Her love for you makes her think of you as still a child."

"Yes, both my parents coddle me. I both love and hate it. I guess I'll just have to wait until they grow up. I told her not to call the police because they won't come if and when there may be something serious that happens. She had agreed to that at least."

"Okay, let's get this show on the road, or we will miss the real show."

CHAPTER 18

The ride into Boston was pleasant since the evening was warm with a cooling breeze that made it the delightful New England weather Jen loved. They talked about what each did during the time they were separated from each other and how each one missed the other with such deep feelings. Since the orange Karmann Ghia stayed at home, they took the rented auto. Jen could slide very close to him on the front seat and feel his body close to hers.

"We are the 'future' as civil rights defenders. How do you think this will all end?" Jen asked.

"Just the way we want it to end—with both of us happily married with two gorgeous children and successful careers. That's how it ends," Brason said confidently.

"I sure hope so, my sweet, handsome man," she said as they arrived at the front door of the Jazz Cavern to leave the car with the valet.

Upon entering the Jazz Cavern, there was a long walkway with walls displaying all the jazz performers like Billie Holiday, who had passed away just a few years before in 1959. Louis 'Satchmo' Armstrong, The Duke, the Dave Brubeck Quartet, and a young Black vocalist, John Mathis, who had presented his talents here at The Jazz Cavern. The lights created the initial excitement before entering the sunken main stage area. The intimate seating at a candlelit table and plush seats invited one to snuggle in to enjoy the performers on center stage. Brason had reserved a table for two near the stage, and the rhythm of the energy in the room sent tingles up Jen's spine as they settled into the comfort of the chairs. The opening act left the stage to voluminous applause. They had missed the opening act.

"With immense pride, please give a very warm welcome to Ms. Carmen McRae."

"Wow, we made it just in time."

"Yes, we are lucky," he whispered to Jen. "And we're especially lucky that the main star is Carmen McRae, one of the most promising vocalist-pianists of the 20th Century. We are in for a performance of one of the most potentially influential jazz artists of our time," he said as he kissed Jen on the cheek. She smiled lovingly at him.

The performance was outstanding, a delightful performance of the evening with the most incredible vocal delivery and improvisational skills one could encounter. It was an education in vocal production and astounding manipulation of vocal agility. Jen was thrilled, and Brason smiled as he saw how happy she appeared.

"As much as I wish she had come out for an encore, I'm glad she didn't, because it's getting late and we must go."

"She was extraordinary. I wish she had done an encore, but I also wish I could sing like that," Jen remarked wistfully.

"You're pretty good already. Keep studying and experimenting, and who knows what will happen. But now, we must hurry because my friends are waiting for us at the Ally Dance Club, a ballroom just down the street on the first block of Boylston Street, to meet my friends Thatcher and Jona. I think you will like them," he said as he helped her up from the table and held her hand to exit the area. As they walked through the long walkway toward the exit, a female voice called out: "Brason, you little devil! What are you doing in Boston?"

"Please, Jen, give me a minute?"

"Yes, of course."

After a brief time, Brason returned, but not before Jen heard the louder portion of the conversation when Brason said to the woman, "Well, I'm very sorry, but we must move on."

"Is everything okay?" Jen asked as Brason approached the valet with his ticket.

"Yes, I'll explain later. Let's just get to the next exciting event."

CHAPTER 19

The ride to The Ally Dance Club was just a few blocks from the jazz club. It was in an alley off Boylston Street. At the entrance of the alley, the valet was set up to take their car as patrons walked down the alley to the red entrance door of The Alley Dance Club, where a very large Black bouncer stood ready to tend to any issues that might occur. Jen had never been on the other side of the Black and White divide, nor in such close proximity, but here she was in the very heart of the social Black culture of Boston's Black community. The most Jen had ventured into mixed-race dating was to date, for a short time, a kind, thoughtful, and intelligent Black Captain stationed at Hanscom Airfield. They would have dinner and dance at the Officers' Club on Saturdays when he was off duty, and she had some time. He was fun. He was adorable, and he liked her well enough to ask her to go home to Georgia with him. That seemed to end the relationship when both realized the impossibility of the situation.

The relationship with Brason was so different. Brason was like a Category 3 hurricane with uncontrollable energy and excitement in every moment of his life. All Jen wanted was to be with him in their private bubble. Now, all these people made her apprehensive. She had heard many stories that caused her to be concerned about mixed-race life.

"Good evening, and welcome to The Alley Club," the big man greeted.

"Good evening, I am here as the guest of Thatcher Riley. I am Attorney General Brason Washington."

"Please follow our hostess. She will take you to Mr. Riley's table."

"Right this way, Mr. Washington. I believe your party is waiting for you," she said as they followed this amazingly beautiful young Black girl with a charming voice to the Thatcher's table.

"Hey there, buddy, how the hell are you? We can't believe you're here, but I can see the reason why you're here. She's lovely."

The environment, the music, and the people overwhelmed Jen. She had never been in such an exotic place. The area where they sat had individual circular tables with soft, deeply cushioned seats under enormous canopies of fabric, much like parachutes, airy and backlit for dramatic intensity. The fresh, flowered pots of hanging plants made it feel as if they were in a plush garden. All this overlooked the expansive dance floor, where bodies moved to the pulsating beats of the new sounds of the '60s and what the popular clubs played.

Brason began the introductions.

"Jen, I would like you to meet my college roommate, Thatcher Riley—one hellava civil rights attorney."

"It's a pleasure to meet you, Thatcher."

"It's my pleasure. Allow me to introduce my fiancé, Julie Sanders."

"It's so nice to meet you," Jen replied.

"And this… this is Jona Jackson, the meanest, bestest trial lawyer in our class, and in any courtroom in the United States of America."

"Well, I know where to go if I ever need good lawyers. It's very nice to meet you."

"This is Jane Black."

"Hello, Jane, are you also an attorney?" Jen asked.

"No, I'm a dance major studying at the Boston Conservatory of Music and planning to go to Juilliard."

"Oh, yes, I'm familiar. I went to the New England Conservatory at one point to study, but I knew I would never make it as a concert pianist, so I left and went to study law. I often took some dance classes at BCM."

After all the introductions, everyone sat down. Brason ordered drinks for them. Thatcher ordered another round, saying to Brason, "Come on, guys, you have to catch up. I believe this is your first time at The Alley? We hope you like it."

Brason and Jen smiled at each other, knowing how little either of them drank, while the conversation, filled with such joy and laughter, grew exuberant and loud with the excitement of being together.

"Yes, I'm impressed," Jen remarked.

The drinks came. They toasted one another with raised drinks. "Cheers to friendships, health, wealth, and lots of great fun with friends forever."

"Okay, guys, let's dance!" shrieked Jane, who had been bouncing in her seat since the beginning of the song. The disc jockey was excellent, and the music flowed seamlessly from one song to the next without missing a beat. The dance floor was crowded; it was all free-style dancing. The music beat through Jen's body as it pulsed its beat in decibels so loud it almost hurt her ears. Any conversation was impossible. True self-expression was erotically displayed on the dance floor. Jen gave her best sensual moves, though limited, to show

how well she could fit into the setting. It was one of those long, extended versions disc jockeys loved to play. By the end of almost forty-five minutes of high-intensity dancing, they returned to their lovely, quiet hut. However, as they made their way through the crowd to their table, Jen heard some rather loud, angry voices say things that were so upsetting to her and possibly to Thatcher's white fiancé. Things like "… white trash, …whores for Black dicks, … bitches takin' our Black brothers… whites can't raise our children," and the most moving of all, "… go home and leave our men alone."

"Did you hear some of what I heard, Brason?"

"Don't pay any attention to those remarks. They mean nothing to us. We must think above that," he said as he kissed Jen on the cheek.

Thatcher must have heard some of it, though Julie seemed unbothered by what was said. On the other hand, Jen was frightened. But the intimate party continued. Soon, the very large Black bouncer came to their table with a strong suggestion.

"Gentlemen, I think it is time for you to take your ladies to the Sugar Shack for something to eat, as the environment is getting a bit uncomfortable. Our ladies don't appreciate your white dates. Tensions might cause problems, and my job is to ensure that no problems develop. I am terribly sorry."

Brason paid the tab and said good night to Thatcher, Jona, and their dates. The guys talked for a few moments, telling each other that they would soon get together, maybe in New York, where acceptance was a little easier. Brason and Jen walked out of The Alley Dance Club quietly and quickly. Their automobile was waiting at the entrance of the alley, and they were soon safely in their car heading back home.

"Brason, has that ever happened to you before?" Jen asked.

"What—being asked to leave a place? You should only know how many times in my life I have been asked to leave a place and never come back. It's usually in an all-white club. Often, I'm not even allowed in."

"Oh, Brason, I'm so sorry. It hurts me to know that there is such bigotry. When I was young, the Irish kids would call me 'Ghinnie,' or 'mongrel,' which hurt, but I thought that when I grew up, it would have changed. When will it end?"

"I don't know, but I will not allow it to disrupt my plans for a happy life with you. I am truly sorry that you had to experience this. Let's just go home and get into our bubble. It seems to be a safe place."

"Yes, let's go home."

As they pulled into the driveway, the exterior lighting design illuminated the trees and the flowers at the entrance of the property, while the white picket fence created an open invitation to step into the imaginary bubble Brason and Jen envisioned as their safe, loving security spot. The house seemed to welcome the two lovers who retreated home for their hibernation from the ugly world, if only for a few hours, until it was time to say 'Au revoir.'

They each fell into bed, exhausted by the experience of the evening. Jen nestled into Brason's arms, immediately falling into a deep sleep. She had had more excitement in this one day than she had in a very long time. Fortunately, her brain did not formulate the hundreds of questions that usually invaded her early hours of falling asleep. Instead, she simply drifted into a deep sleep in Brason's arms as he, too, disengaged from the world outside and slept in the joy of his love for Jen. Holding this precious, inexperienced young woman in his arms, his need to be close to her was satisfied by her soft, gentle breathing. They would talk at breakfast tomorrow. Both slept deeply and soundly.

CHAPTER 20

The couple woke refreshed to the ever-present singing of birds in the trees just outside the bedroom window. Jen and Brason emerged from the deep sleep of the exhausting night before with a smile and a kiss—the kiss each thought of every morning while they were separated—and they luxuriated in the fact that today they had their bodies together in reality and not imaginary mode. They were thrilled to be together and did not want to get out of bed. Actually, they didn't have to go anywhere until 3 p.m., when it would be time again for Brason to leave for more months of separation.

"Good morning, my little darling, how are you feeling after such a good sleep?"

"My, what an intense night! Actually, the entire evening was intense, but you're here, and I am so happy to wake to your handsome, smiling face. Have I told you today that I love you?"

"No, you have not."

"Well, Mr. Brason Washington, I love and adore you."

"Well, Ms. Jenni, I adore and love you with all my heart," he said as he pulled her close and they kissed the passionate kiss they had been anticipating since last night. The intensity of the two well-rested, energized bodies, mixed and enfolded in the growing love each felt for the other. Jen's soft, white skin draped over the beautifully buffed, bronzed skin of Brason inflamed the two lovers, carrying them to their point of delight, one she had never experienced before. This intensity overwhelmed her.

"I think I could spend the rest of my life right here with you in our bubble," Jen said to Brason as she ran her fingers over his well-coiffed hair and then over his body.

"Okay, let's retire and never leave this property. We'll just stay home, write articles, form civil rights districts on a map, and send our ideas to the NAACP for securing civil rights and reforming the states that continue to ban interracial marriages."

"Yes, it sounds great, but we will need money to live, so that idea is not possible at the moment. But if we go to work, save our money, retire early, then we can be together and work the rest of our lives on civil rights and human rights."

"Sounds good to me," Brason said playfully as he tickled, kissed, and hugged Jen, and they both frolicked together in sheer enjoyment of being together in their bubble.

They made love again and soon fell into another deep, loving sleep. They woke at noon.

"I usually call for room service, but I'll bet we can't do it here!"

"If you say it nicely—I know the chef in this Casa Mia."

"No, my love, I don't want you to work in the kitchen. I saw a neat little restaurant just downtown that I think would be great to go to for brunch. How about it?"

"It sounds good. Would you like to shower?"

"Is that an invitation?"

"It certainly could be, if you wish."

They both playfully rushed to the shower, splashing childishly together.

The shower cleansed their bodies and enriched their souls with the tender lovemaking among the warm drops of the shower, after which they dressed for the warm temperature of the day and the expectation of a ride in Jen's signature orange Karmann Ghia convertible.

It was a grand day. The sun shone brightly over the trees in the backyard. The apple orchard was in flower, indicating that the apples would be ready for the fall picking. There was absolute joy in this little home in the country. Jen, at this moment, was happier than she had ever been because she refused to let any questions of doubt enter her mind. When those doubts arose, she simply held Brason's hand and kissed his cheek. That seemed to push away the negative and embrace the love, at least while he was here. It was not so easy when he was away.

Jen locked up the house, then opened the car door. She began unlatching the convertible cover, and Brason helped place the cover in its proper position over the back seat.

"This should be a lot of fun, Brason," Jen remarked.

"I must tell you. This little orange bug has been the most fun of my life. I purchased this car from a tiny square chart that appeared to be a burnt orange with a black convertible roof, but when I went to pick it up, it was astonishingly orange. All I could think of was that my parents were going to make such a trauma over the color. A good friend who drove me to pick up the car told me that in order to sabotage my mother's attacks on me, which there were sure to be a lot of, if I went into the house exuberantly excited about my new orange car, they would not be able to attack my joy or mock my choice."

"How'd that go?"

"He was absolutely correct. No one ever made fun of my orange car, although Mom teased me by calling me the Head of the City Maintenance Crew, which I thought was very funny. Their trucks were orange colored."

"I guess everyone in the city could tell where you were on any specific day or night."

"Yup, sometimes I'd get to the AG's office, and someone would say, 'Hey, you were at the Rusty Scupper last night. I thought you were going directly home.'"

"Great way to keep an eye on you."

"Well, you don't have to keep an eye on me. Hopefully, I'll always be within eyes' distance someday. So, here we are at the spot you wanted to have brunch or lunch. Ready?"

"They have a great Breakfast Scramble. It's what I had the other day when I came here. Try it. I think you'll like it."

This was one of the few times Jen went to an eatery in her neighborhood. She did grocery shopping, but she would travel closer to the big city to do her restaurant and clothes shopping for a better variety. She also felt a strange tension in the small, intimate, family-run eatery, but she decided that it was probably residual emotions from the events of the night before. They had not discussed that situation and had preferred to just revel in the joy of being together. She was certain it would come up during the hours before he had to leave.

"How about this table?" Jen asked, pointing to a cozy table in the corner by the window that looked out onto another eatery, a bird feeder, where squirrels scampered about gathering the seeds meant for the birds.

"This is the exact table I chose. It's fun watching those cagey squirrels take their food as they hang from the feeder with one arm. I find them fascinating, just like acrobats," he said as they sat to read the menu and order brunch.

They enjoyed the healthy omelets they ordered, which served as both breakfast and lunch. They talked mostly about what each had been doing in the months they had not seen each other, seeming to intentionally steer clear of the underlying serious issue of being asked to leave a club because they were a mixed couple, and a serious conflict had brewed with an unpleasant resolve. When they ate every morsel of their Breakfast Scramble, paid the check, and left the restaurant, it was time to walk.

"How about we walk and talk?" suggested Brason.

"Where? Here is a stretch of small shops, or we can take a short drive to the really big mall, where there are upscale stores."

"No, I just want to get the feel of this small town and the people that we will have to face as we become a couple."

"So far, I haven't seen anything to indicate that we must be cautious. My neighbors still wave 'Hello' and watch over me protectively. Just as the neighbor who called the police, thinking someone was breaking into my house."

"It has been all positive on your end of the spectrum, but The Alley Dance Club was a debacle, which I have never experienced before. I must admit, I'm quite upset by it."

"That is what sometimes happens," Brason reminded her.

"Will it happen everywhere, as we become more visible?" Jen questioned.

"I've always believed that when we are true in our determination, the rest of the world will follow us."

"Your theory might be incorrect. There might be even more hate in the world than I can imagine."

"My darling, hate is out there; it is evil, dangerous, and totally unfair."

By this time, they had walked down one side of the street where haberdashery stores displayed summer fashions to this small town, and up the other side where small specialty food shops sliced their delicious imported cheeses for tasting. Jen had never spent any time in the downtown of this city, but with Brason, it seemed rather charming instead of 'geographically undesirable.' Now, she actually found her small town geographically quite desirable, though she noticed frowns on the faces of a few passers-by.

"It looks like we are getting close to my having to leave for the airport. My flight leaves at 3 p.m., and I am expected back at my office on time tomorrow. I have many things to do before that, so we will have to get back home for my luggage and the car."

"Oh, that's right. I didn't give it a thought. I was planning to drive you to the airport, but that won't be necessary, will it? You have to return the car," Jen stated.

"Yes, you are correct, again," he said as he kissed her cheek and put his arm around her waist while they approached where the Ghia was parked.

At home, the two lovers made love with intensity that would last until July, or until the next time he visited. They promised to keep in close touch through the next weeks until Jen told Brason whether she would be coming to the Washington Family Fourth of July Jamboree. If Jen could arrange it, Brason would send her the round-trip ticket.

"Remember, as soon as you decide that you are coming to meet my family on July 4, I will send you your ticket. Tell me the time and the day you want to travel. You may come any day of the entire week. Our family takes all that time to prepare. You will stay with Grandma Washington in her home. She has six bedrooms, but I will sleep in Great-Grandpa's room. He's so much fun, and some of the family will be in the other bedrooms."

"Okay, I'll let you know as soon as I can figure out what my family's plans will be for that weekend. They haven't told me anything, but I could bet that they will be going out on the yacht for what will definitely be a 'bashingly fun time,' as everyone jokingly always says."

"Jen, thank you for a pleasurable weekend, though short."

"Brason, my darling, it might have been short, but it was packed with some thought-provoking moments."

"Yes, thoughts that will mull around in my mind long after we have said goodbye."

"I, too, shall have many thoughts floating in my mind while you are gone, but we both must look not only at our lives together, but at our careers, our families, and our future children. What we decide will definitely affect all of them."

"Then we shall take the necessary time to be certain that we make the right decisions," Brason said as he pulled Jen close to him and they kissed goodbye in the foyer before he left the house. Jen followed him to the car as he unlocked the trunk and placed his suitcases inside. They kissed again before he got into the car, backed out, and lowered the window to wave goodbye to a tearful Jen. Then he drove away.

The taillights of the automobile indicated that Brason stopped at the stop sign at the end of the street and then disappeared with a right turn in the direction that would lead him to the airport. He was gone, and Jen was alone to think about all she had experienced to date in the relationship she and Brason shared. Jen's emotions were very tangled. All she knew was that when she was with him in her little bubble, she was deliriously happy, but it was apparent that when they were out in the public eye, she was not as comfortable or as happy as she should be.

"It's probably best if I don't talk to Dad about Brason yet. Maybe just work on Mom until I have actually decided that I would marry Brason," Jen wisely thought.

Jen was now alone in her quiet home. Brason left his presence behind in the house. It lasted for weeks, followed by the emptiness Jen felt in her soul. It brought an emptiness that Jen had never experienced. She had mostly loved being alone in her house, but since Brason, her life did not feel quite the same. The only constant was the law and her career, but it seemed no longer enough to fill the space.

CHAPTER 21

"Good morning, Nancy. How was your weekend?"

"Great, the baby was sick with a cold, and we had to rush to the Children's Hospital, and my six-year-old fell while attempting to climb up the cabinet for some candies I hid from him. He has a gash on his forehead. Fortunately, he didn't need stitches. Otherwise, nothing very exciting happened. We absolutely don't have time for any afternoon delight, if you know what I mean."

"Yes, afternoon delight, I know what that means. Sometimes singles have some of those afternoons as well."

"So, tell me, did you have lots of delight in the afternoons this weekend?"

"Some, but the weekend was wilder than I ever imagined it could get. You know I'm usually quiet and like the peace of my home, the yard, the apple orchard, and my music, but this weekend was like a July 4th explosion every minute. Never could I have thought it would be me in the middle of such strange happenings."

"Okay, happenings? What kind of strange happenings? Let it all out."

(Jen began extolling all the precious moments of the incredible weekend of Brason's visit before getting into the real issues…)

"We had so much fun. We went for brunch at a little hole-in-the-wall restaurant in my small downtown. He was handsome, charming, and loving. I love him so much, but I must admit it was a stress-filled weekend, especially when I found the police at my house when I returned from my mother's, then at an all-Black dance club where we met his college roommates, another friend, and their girlfriends. It was shortly after a dance and a few drinks we were asked by a very large, muscular bouncer to leave the club for fear that some 'crazy stuff' could break out."

"First police were at your house, and then you were kicked out of a club. Why? What did you do? What crazy stuff?"

"Nan, I don't understand anything anymore."

"Well, my 'Pollyanna' friend, do you think that life for a mixed couple in this day and age will be easier? Do you think the public will accept the social mixing of races that apparently is moving forward? I think you are wrong, but I will never stand in the way of Cupid's arrow. If and when the public begins accepting the social mixing that seems to be coming our way, many laws will need to be created for your protection, but will they? How long will we have to wait?"

"Yes, you may very well be right, but the subject is far too deep to discuss now. It will have to wait until tomorrow. I've got to sit in on that desegregation meeting with my assistant, Attorney General. How about lunch tomorrow? I'll tell you the whole story?"

"Sure. Just leave me in the middle… go now!"

(Next day at lunch in the Boston Common, Jen and Nan are talking)

"Oh, Nan, I'm so happy. I finally got a good night's sleep last night."

"Well, I'm happy you slept well. I couldn't sleep last night. I was so eager to hear more of the Ally Dance Club story. Tell me about the 'crazy stuff' you began to tell but never finished."

"Nan, we got kicked out of the Ally Dance Club."

"What? The Alley Dance Club? What the heck were you doing to get 'kicked out' or even asked to leave a club? Not YOU!"

"Well, yes, me, Brason, his college roommate, and his white date. We were all asked to leave, politely, of course, because there might be a disturbance brought on by the two Black men for bringing their white dates to the all-Black club."

"Oh, my gosh. What did Brason say about that?"

"He was so blasé about it. That shocked me. I expected more of an angry retaliation… a defense of our right to be there or something. But… NOTHING! He just thanked the bouncer and said, 'It's late, and we had better call it a night.' I was frightened because I heard the evil remarks from some of the people at tables we passed while we were escorted out of the club."

"What kind of remarks?"

"They were those horrible name-calling words that hurt… 'white whores taking our Black men… go home, bitch… find your own white guys… white trash women cannot raise our Black male children or even our Black female children… to live in this world as Blacks.' There was so much hate in those remarks that I was happy we were leaving, but Brason simply smiled as he thanked the bouncer for doing his job. Then we said goodnight to Brason's former roommate, and we left."

"Did you discuss with Brason what happened?"

"Yes, I asked him if he had ever been asked to leave a club before?"

"To him, that must have been a funny question. Did he laugh?"

"Yes, he laughed. 'Some wouldn't even let me in. It was not so much funny, but rather it was not unusual,' he answered."

"He told me that he is often asked to leave places. He has become accustomed to that kind of treatment, and he has learned to live above it. However, I'm not certain I can handle it with such charm and self-assuredness as he does. I was so tempted to respond to those remarks I heard as I walked through the crowd, but the odds of winning were slim to impossible, and being hugely outnumbered, we could have caused a very dangerous conflict."

"Wise thinking. Good choice."

"We had better get back to work. Honestly, I was so angry and very frightened."

"Oh, Jen, I'm sorry, but you must know that it will continue to happen as long as this desegregation and voting rights stuff is on the plate of our White House. President Johnson is following in the steps, I believe, of President John F. Kennedy, to press forward until he gets a bill that he can sign for the Voting Rights Act and one for the Civil Rights movement."

"Do you think that will change life? Will the hate go away? Will acceptance of social mixing become commonplace? Will we be safe to choose our mates regardless of each other's backgrounds or preferences? Or the right to vote and uphold the freedoms promised in the Constitution?

"I'm not certain, Jen. You know that the 15th Amendment was ratified in 1870 to give citizens the right to vote, to not be denied or abridged by the U.S. or any state for their color or previous condition of servitude. Actually, we're still fighting for those freedoms."

"I know. I can't help but think that we are still quite far away from the utopia that he apparently felt we would be able to carve out for ourselves, but I am not at all certain."

"Give it time. You will begin to understand just what you must face if you go in his direction. You will have to consider how your children will have to fight for their position in life. You will have to help them understand yours, too."

"I was humiliated to a point that I was unable to tell Brason how terribly shocked I felt. I became so numb that I never realized how all my feelings were frozen. I didn't know how I was going to get through the remaining hours of the weekend. I simply followed Brason obediently and trusted his view that things would get better. He apparently was comfortable letting it go since it happens to him often."

"Well, you did get through the weekend with no argument, right? Now you can feel whatever it is that you feel. Relax, take a deep breath… okay, now think. Just what do you feel?"

(Pauses to think.)

"I feel… angry… I feel very angry… extremely angry… that people I don't even know are managing to influence my life with their bigotry, fear, and hate… and that's on both sides—the Blacks and the whites. I will have to fight for everything Brason and I will have in our lives—a continual fight to achieve what is rightly our children's or ours. I don't know if I can manage it for myself, let alone for children I don't even have yet."

"It sounds as if you need to speak to someone who can guide you on this one."

"Yes, my grandfather. He is in touch with all the pains of adjusting to other cultures and people who caused Italians the same type of problems when they first came to this country. I'll see him this weekend. I'm going out on the water with my family and their best friends, the Salernos."

"Will Robert, Jr. be there?"

"Probably. It will be good to see him. We had so much fun together growing up. His family had a house at the beach, and all the kids would swim off the dock and hang out playing games and just talking. Bobbie, as his mom calls him, and I would spend hours talking about what we wanted to do when we grew up. He always wanted to be a real estate attorney and grow his fortune by buying large tracts of property to sell to contractors, especially in Colorado. His focus is to fulfill his dream by developing a grand mountain resort with lodges, cabins, and ski trails. He skied in Vermont, New Hampshire, and Maine growing up, but he had bigger ideas."

"He certainly sounds ambitious."

"He's brilliant, handsome, has a rich pedigree and is kind."

"Sounds like he's a good, safe catch. Your mom must think so, too."

"There's more, but I've got to go. I have a meeting in 15 minutes. Can we have lunch again tomorrow so I can tell you about the worst things that happened on this fun weekend?"

"Worst things? Sure, but how worse can it get? Oh, yay, another sleepless night."

Jen went to her meeting with a smile on her face, but with a worried heart. After the meeting, she finished her work and left for class. She was tired, so she stayed at the studio for the night to avoid the long ride back to the country.

CHAPTER 22

The week went faster than Jen had anticipated; however, she had not heard from Brason, nor had she been able to reach him anytime she called him. It appeared this was the way they would have to live their lives because their careers would take them away from each other weeks at a time, even if they were married.

"I'm beginning to think that this will be an impossible love affair," Jen said, crying in her Ghia at the end of the week, deciding whether to stop at the Rusty Scupper or just go home. She had not heard from Brason, and she was unable to get in touch with him all week. She realized Brason had a full-time position as AG and that any campaigning had to be done off the clock. Jen decided the Scupper was the place to put herself back on track to deal with this thing called the 'Brason Love Affair.'

She wiped her eyes, dashed a fresh splash of perfume and a new sweep of lipstick, and headed the orange Ghia toward the Scupper. It was a wise decision, for who she saw right away… Ed… the engineer. They had a drink, talked a while, and made arrangements to go to lunch together the following week. They exchanged numbers, and Jen was off on her road back to the country where she was not quite as safe as usual. It was the weekend, and as usual, Jen's parents were going out on the yacht with the Salernos.

(Jen entered the locked country house to a ringing phone.)

"Hello. Hi, Mom. How are things? Ya, of course, it has been a very busy week. No, I haven't been able to reach my illustrious friend, but I certainly will tonight. But, Mom, what are you guys doing this weekend? I think I need some R&R with family and friends. Oh, fine. I always like to have Robert Jr. join us. No problem. What time Saturday? Okay, I'll see you at 10:00 a.m. at the dock. Great, goodbye for now."

"I guess I'll attempt to reach Brason," she thought as she sat to dial his telephone number.

Jen's phone was on the wall near the kitchen table, allowing for telephone conversations to last considerably longer than if one were standing. Jen pulled up a chair, sat down, and dialed. When Brason finally answered, he was out of breath.

"Hi, darling, I heard the phone ringing, and I had to run from another part of the campaign office. So, my dear, how did you get through the week?"

"It wasn't difficult, but there were just so many questions for which I have no answers. I guess it would be easier if we were handling all of life's idiosyncrasies together. It's the separation that seems impossible for me, Brason."

"I know, but we will manage through all the 'heavy problems,' and we'll be ready for all the intricate hoops we'll have to jump through to get to where we want to go."

"I've been trying to sit and talk with my folks, but there always seems to be something else more important in their life than my life. I'm going out on the water with everyone, so after a few drinks, maybe I can get my dad alone. I can then begin to talk with him."

"That sounds like a risky approach to a serious discussion, so be careful with all the others there."

"Yes, I will. We never said much to each other about what happened the night at The Alley, so I thought we might talk about that soon?"

"Of course, we can talk about anything you wish. I miss you very much, and it will be a month or so before I can see you again. Have you considered the July 4th family cookout?"

"Yes, and I should know by the beginning of next week how and what my family has planned. I am almost certain that I will be able to make it. I had planned to submit my application to take the Bar exam in July, but I'm afraid I won't be totally ready, so I'm thinking of taking it in February. Our State offers it only for those two months."

"When you come to meet my family, I promise I will put aside some time for us to go over some of what you must study. I will help you. I miss you very much and really need to have you with me. I can't explain how empty I feel without you. I liked going to the little town for coffee while you were doing other things away from home. It felt kinda 'married' in a way for which I have no explanation."

"Well, I feel lost without having you around. Your strength seems to help me be strong, but I must admit that night at The Alley Dance Club really gave me insight into what our world might be like. Would the Blacks ask me to leave places because I am white? Will you be asked to leave or never even be admitted to places because you are Black? I felt humiliated and worthless. I was unable to defend myself against such odds."

"My darling, you must learn to put those negative feelings aside. We win by both of us being hugely successful, and by that, we win. Our children will be schooled in excellent public schools, and our strength will be displayed by our achievements."

"What if my parents don't accept what we plan? What if they cannot see any good coming from our being together? They see discrimination as the secret ingredient that is deeply rooted in the bigotry that exists. There is actual hate. Hate for the Blacks taking over from white America, and hate for white women taking their Black men. If hate is at the base of it all, how will our country ever get through it?"

"My darling, the only way we can get through it is by actually facing the hate with love and joy of that love. When we do, we achieve some of the promises of Dr. King in his 'I Have a Dream' speech. Also, please read the extraordinary yet long letter he wrote while incarcerated in Birmingham Jail. It tells us much about what we must do."

"Okay, I will read that and everything that will help me be 50% of your life that I will face. I am sorry we did not discuss this before in person, but in our bubble, it was not the place to discuss such hurt. All I wanted to do was make love to you and tell you how much I loved you."

"If you love me as much as you say you do, then you must find the strength to speak to your dad and tell him exactly what we plan."

"Plans? I'm having the worst experience of my life approaching my dad about what I plan to do with our relationship, since all the plans of my life have been made by him, almost all my life."

"Yes, I understand, but now it is time for you to take a stance and let him know what we plan."

"Braking, just how do you see the plans working?"

"First of all, you must visit my family. See what takes place in a loving environment. Yes, there is deep pain all Blacks hold within their being; however, in our family, we have all learned to channel that hate from those who have nothing to do with our history."

"Do you mean slavery?"

"Yes, of course. You and your family had nothing to do with using, owning, or believing that slavery was an acceptable process for the production of goods, did you?"

"No, my grandparents came to the United States as immigrants from Italy. We had to survive in whatever way we could. My great-grandfather was a stonecutter and cement worker in Milano, Italy. He taught my grandfather his trade, and grandpa became a contractor doing concrete work for the City of Boston. His brother bought some chicks and became a chicken farmer—and quite successful, I must say. Therefore, I don't carry the guilt that some people are talking about."

"Then it should be easier for you to talk with your dad about what we see for ourselves in this crazy world."

"I suppose it should be, but somehow intellectually I see it clearly, but emotionally I am unable to come up with the words that make it possible for me to defend my point."

"Well, if you expect to become a successful attorney winning your point of view in a hostile environment, it will be the best exercise for your future."

"I guess you're right. I will use it as an exercise in expanding the education of my law practice as a lesson in successfully changing others' points of view on specific issues over to my point of view. It will be a well-learned lesson."

"When you come to our July celebration, I promise we will take some time to formulate a defense attorney's dialogue on how to approach your dad."

"You promise? Do you really think it might work? Do you see how much I need to be with you to have the strength I must have to face the personal problems I have?"

"Strength is what you must have and the ability to keep feelings contained and love to surface to the top of everything that we want for us."

"I, too, promise that I will keep a positive attitude and build a wall of defense that cannot be penetrated. I love you so much that I believe that all you say can come true."

"Yes, my sweet, just be positive and write down your hesitations. When we see each other the next time, we will be closer to being together because of your strength. For now, I must say good night and wish you a productive week."

"Yes, my love, I will do all that you say. I look forward to connecting with you by phone and sharing my thoughts and deeds with you."

"Now, have a good week. We will talk. Know that I love you very much and have spoken to my grandparents, and they are so excited about your coming to stay with us on the 4th. Until next we speak, just remember, I love you beyond the words I say."

"Goodnight, my love. Carry me in your heart every minute. I love you."

Each hung up the phone. Brason still had papers, notes, dates to record, and so much that had to be done for his campaign that he did not go to sleep until 2 a.m. His wake-up call was at 5 a.m. With only a few hours of sleep, Brason had to be ready for another long day of campaigning. He was really good at a 10-minute snatch of downtime to regenerate his energy.

Jen, on the other hand, turned on her music, put a log on the fire for atmosphere, not heat. She dimmed the lights and sang her songs of the heart, singing along with Dionne Warwick and Burt. It was another bubble that Jen could envelop herself in when she had serious decisions to make or just to leave the real world and disappear into her imaginary world. There she was, safe and happy.

CHAPTER 23

Jen woke to a dreary, rainy, high-humidity day. The weather was contrary to how she felt. Today, she was exuberant and full of energy. She hit the books for several hours until lunch, when she took a break and made a chicken salad with iced tea for her lunch. The rain gave a gentle tapping sound against the roof, creating a cozy feeling of safety in the house, and the flowers danced happily in their garden design.

The study was going really well. Jen met Robert for lunch several afternoons at the Yacht Club. She had begun to rely on her comfortable relationship with Robert to ask him on many occasions for team study time on various sections of the law. They would spend time discussing her work. He was patient with her and impressed with her tenacity in the rules of law.

They had lunch a few times until one day he said, "I have a formal dinner to attend with some potential realtors on a land deal I am putting together for a ski resort in Aspen and would really like you to be my date."

"A date, Robert?"

"Yes, do you think you can handle it?"

"I have a lovely gown and possibly a free night, but I'm not certain I can… but are you sure… a date?"

"Yes, it is the weekend of July 4th, so put that on your calendar."

"Oh no, I am supposed to make a decision to go visit Brason's family on that weekend."

"Brason? Who's Brason?"

"Remember I told you about the Attorney General I met at the AG's Conference a few months ago?"

"No, I don't recall. Are you serious about him?"

"Well, here's the entire story." And she told him all about Brason. "It's just like when we were kids. I'd tell you everything about every boy I liked or every boy who liked me. And, that's the end of my story about Brason." She intentionally neglected mentioning the most important characteristic of her man... his Blackness.

"Okay, I understand. You just met this extraordinary guy a few months ago, and he swept you off your perch. I will say what I would say back when we were kids, 'no one likes you more than I do,' and you would laugh and tell me we were best buddies forever and ever."

"Well, we are, aren't we?"

"Yes, of course. So, will you be my date for this event, or does that harm our buddies' stature?"

"Of course not. I like you, and I always have. I also value your wise judgment. I haven't fully decided whether to go or not to Brason's annual family gathering. Can you give me a week or so to decide?"

"That will be fine, but remember I must have a date for this event."

"I will, and I'll let you know what I decide, okay?"

"Fine. I've got to get back to my office, so we will talk whenever." They got the check and left the club.

Robert went back to his office, and Jen went for more team study with the kids at school.

The weekend passed, but no call from Brason, and Jen called the personal number several times throughout the weekend, but there was never an answer this week. He must be really busy with work and campaigning. Frustration was beginning to set in for Jen, but she realized that when careers are flourishing, free time is minimal. She would have to accept this as part of their life together as singles, and unfortunately, the same would be true when married, too.

After Sunday Mass, Jen went to her mom's house for lunch. Jen really wanted to talk to her Grandpa, who had not been feeling quite himself. He was a strong old guy and still as sharp as the sharpest tool in his toolbox, as he liked to say. The walk into her mom's house was filled with the aroma of the Italian pasta sauce stewing in its pot, permeating the air and stimulating the juices of their hungry stomachs because they had continued the process of fasting from midnight to after communion in the Mass.

"Hopefully, more things will change in the future," Jen thought as she followed grandpa into the garden, and her mom went to her room to change into the clothes she wears around the house. Dad sat in his chair, reading the Sunday paper and arguing with the comments on the paper. The dialogue between Dad and the air in the room escalated to irritation and then anger. Left to himself, Dad enjoyed this repartee.

"Grandpa, I would really like to ask you for some advice. Can we talk in the garden and in confidence?"

"Jennita, I always have time for you. Watching you grow to the beautiful, intelligent, and kind woman you are is my joy."

"Grandpa, I've met an incredible man. He is handsome, educated, successful, and considerate. I met him at the Attorney General's Conference a few months ago, and we really hit it off. I like him, but distance is our nemesis, and a year from this coming November, he plans to run for governor of his state. I graduate in May of the same year, and he wants me to marry him."

"That sounds very exciting, but do you love him? Unless you love him without reservation, it doesn't matter how wonderful he is; the marriage will never work."

"I'm not certain when he is away, but when I am with him in our little bubble, it seems like a wonderful dream."

"Remember, some dreams turn into nightmares." They both laughed. "Like poor Uncle Carminuch. It was a love—a dream—that filled his life with pain and ultimately took his life. But forgive me, Jennita, I didn't mean to interrupt your story. If you like him, I am certain he is all you say. Now, tell me the issue that is bothering you."

"Do you think that people from different cultures can make a life and bring up children that will be healthy and happy?"

"I suppose it's possible if both parties have the same basic core values and beliefs. Do you know him well enough to know who he really is? A few months does not give you enough time to know that, I don't think."

"Tell me about how my mom, your daughter, came to you before she married Dad."

"First, I will tell you about your grandma, bless her soul. She was born in the same little village in Italy as me, and we were good friends. I was an only child. She was one of cinque bambini, ma che bella ragazzina. Si chiamava Maria e aveva una bella voce… come una angela. Lei era il mio cuore e la mia anima."

"Si, Nonno, so quanto amavi la nonna. I know how much you loved Nonna. I don't think I have reached that point in my relationship with this man. His name is Brason Washington. I don't know if love is strong enough to combat what we have to face as an interracial couple."

"Che interracial? Boy-girl couple, si?"

"Yes, Nonno, a boy and a girl, but a Black boy and a white girl."

"Dio mio. Dio mlo, mi amor. Your father will be very upset. He will raise the roof with his bellowing. Your mother cry in pain but will try to understand. Your father will be angry and carry on. As for me, I would prefer that you look at this situation as if it were a purely legal problem. Stack the facts and the emotions on opposite sides and see what you come up with. When I came to this country with your nonna, I didn't know much about what we would face. I knew that as an immigrant, I would have to do twice the workload and work twice as hard for less pay than any other man. The Irish seemed to be the ones moving up the power chain. Our turn at advancing was years away. The 'blue bloods of Boston' were the mayors and the government people; the Irish, since they spoke English, were who the police worked with, and some for the politicians. The Italians were busy working to construct buildings and grow families. We worked hard to provide food, shelter, clothing, and education for our children. True, there was the element of Mafioso among some Italians, but they were in combat with the bad, unlawful leaders of our state for the protection of their Italian immigrants. Just because we are Italian does not mean we were part of the Mafia. However, it is impossible to change people's perception even if they are willing to have a serious discussion. Only through education and empathy are we able to get past bigotry."

"You are right, Grandpa." She paused in thought. "Thanks, Nonno, I think I will take your suggestion and draw up a diagram placing all the positive elements on one side and negatives on the other side. Then challenge each one separately and intermingle them and see what I come up with."

"Best idea, my darling little girl. Ti amo."

"Me too, Nonno."

"Lunch is ready," Jen's mom called from the kitchen.

"Time to have lunch, Nonno. Thanks for everything."

CHAPTER 24

Jen left her parents carrying containers filled with food for the week. When she got home, she called Robert to ask if he had time for some "lawyer talk." And as always, he was ready to set down whatever he was working on and give time to Jen. He was especially interested in this new guy she called Brason. Who was he? Was he real? Had Jen really fallen in love with him, or was it just that "girly infatuation" with a new, exciting guy? What Robert didn't know and should not have overlooked was that sex with Brason was more than Jen had ever experienced.

"Sure, Jen. Would you like to come to my place, or would you rather I come to yours?"

"If you don't mind, I would like you to come to mine."

"What time would you like to do this? I'm in the middle of some documents and drawings, but I can be there about 2:30 or 3:00 p.m. How's that?"

"That would be perfect." *"Oh, there's that word,"* and she thought about Brason.

Jen hung up the phone, put some soft, mellow music on, and sat down with a pad and pencil to begin the outline for her "lawyering" talks with Robert. She wanted to use her newly acquired skills to put this together, as Nonno suggested. Of course, Robert would have a clearer vision on this subject with details far better than she would be able to do without him. Without realizing it, Jen had depended a great many times on Robert, her best friend since they were just kids, diving off the deck at his summerhouse on the river, or sailing at the Yacht

Club in his Class B Comet sailboat. They were always in each other's lives. How would it be when that was no longer the situation? Jen put down her pen and went to her favorite spot in her living room to look out the window at the flowers and think about her life. She soon fell asleep.

She woke to the sound of the doorbell ringing. It was Robert. She looked at her watch. It was 2:45. Robert was always on time or early. Jen gave a call. "I'm coming."

"Hey, did I wake you?"

"Ya, I guess I fell asleep for a bit. I've been studying and so mixed up that I am exhausted every day."

"Well, that's no way to live. But I brought something that will make life a little mellower while we talk… what did you call it… lawyering?" he said as he produced a fine bottle of wine with a small tray of cheese and crackers.

"Yes, Robert, I want to talk about my new friend, Brason."

"Oh, yay. Brason, the mystery guy you've talked about. Do you need a lawyer for him? What did he do?"

"No, Robert, he hasn't done anything to need an attorney. He *is* an attorney. As a matter of fact, he is a State Attorney General."

"Well, you went to the top. Good girl."

"Stop, Robert! I need your lawyering qualities to help me prepare a successful Venn Diagram."

"That should be fun. Let's get to it." Robert took out his long, yellow legal pad and placed at the top of the page the words "Venn Diagram" and drew its shape of two circles overlapping in the middle. "Okay, are you ready?"

"Yes, I am," Jen said as she poured some wine into two lovely crystal stem glasses and put some crackers with cheese on a plate for each to have.

Robert was so expert in putting difficult issues into simple questions as he began to fill in the diagram to reach a factual solution.

"I think the top two are family and education. Where do you lie on these two issues? Have you discussed your families together? That is a very important subject, but each of you must discuss your decision with your immediate families."

"No, we haven't begun to talk about our families. As a matter of truth, Robert, I haven't told my mother or father about Brason except to say how wonderful he is and how much we like each other."

"Well, that's not doing anything to move this relationship forward. Why haven't you told at least your mom? She would certainly be the first one to talk with."

"No, I've talked with Nonno, but he has told me to set down on a sheet of paper somewhat like we are doing now. He told me to take out the emotion and put down the facts, especially the facts that will not change."

"Let's forget about the Venn Diagram and go with just a list of what must be discussed and what you know and don't know about this guy. Okay?"

"Yes, let's do it."

"What is the major discerning issue of this relationship? The constant?"

"I'm white, and he is Black."

(Robert was in disbelief and shocked…)

"Oh, my heavens, Jen. You know that I have no prejudices, so Black and white, gay or straight, I make no judgment. You could not have picked a more difficult constant to deal with. Your dad will certainly be very upset and possibly disown you. You will smash all his loving plans for your life into tiny pieces, never able to be put together again. But for now, let's first evaluate the differences and the likeness issues, then look at those things that cannot be changed."

Together, Robert and Jen prepared a list of issues that would have to be discussed and resolved with each of the lovers, their families, and even their friends. It was a rather long list with racial differences at the top of the list. At the end of two hours, Jen was tired, and Robert was no longer interested in playing a part in Jen's decision. By now, all the crackers and cheese were gone, and the wine bottle was empty.

"You know the way I feel about you, Jen, and although I have not pressured you to date me, I have always hoped that you might one day look upon me as a potential life partner. We have so much in common. Your parents love me as my parents love you, and I have loved you for all the days that I can remember. So, I must now stop. You have enough information and some important questions for which you must find the answers, especially some of those issues which you are not clear about. I only want to say that I don't think that this man will make you happy, especially if your dad, who, I am certain, will virtually throw you out of the family, does not give his blessing. I believe that the main question you must answer is: Is your love for Brason deep enough and strong enough to win the many battles you and your family will have to face during these tumultuous times in civil rights and human rights? Will you survive it well, without the support of your family?"

"You are right, Robert. Those questions supersede any others because if my parents are not happy with my life, there is no life for me without them."

"Jen, I think I'm going to leave now. The wine is gone with the crackers and cheese. I've helped as much as I really want to help. This puts me in an uncomfortable position because I like you a lot, and I'm not happy about this guy. I think it is just an infatuation that has caused you so much confusion. It is a sweet, short love story, but it is not a lifelong love story for my best friend, Jen. So, I'm going home to leave you to think about what you are planning for your future. It is time for you to sit with Brason and discuss your future. Not me."

"Robert, please, not a word to your mother, father, or mine. I will tell my folks when I am ready. Thank you for your kindness and your help," she said as she leaned to give him a kiss on the cheek. He turned at just that moment, and their lips met. Robert's passion, enhanced by the wine and the sleepy afternoon together with Jen, flowed through the simple brushing of lips into a passionate kiss that left Jen's head spinning in a direction that she had never ever felt for Robert. Life did play strange tricks on people.

Awkwardly, Robert straightened himself and simply stated, "Call me when you decide what you will do. I guess I've not been much help, but we'll see each other soon."

Robert had not left the driveway before the phone rang with a call from Brason.

"Hello, Brason," Jen said as she shook off the spell that lingered after Robert's kiss. She had never seen whatever it was coming.

"Yes, it's me. It feels like we haven't seen each other for years, and you know I can't bear being away from you. Whatcha been doin'?"

"Studying and getting ready for finals. I miss you, Brason. When can we see each other again?" Jen asked in a rather sad tone. "The time moves so slowly, and trying to reach you can be impossible."

"I miss you very much. I know how difficult it is right now, but things will get better, I promise. So, have you decided to come to visit my family for the 4th of July family reunion?"

"Yes, I have given it a great deal of thought. I am planning to visit the Washington family reunion," she responded, without giving any thought to the invitation that Robert extended for the same weekend. "Do you think your folks will be ready to take me on?"

"You, my sweet little pumpkin, will be an easy-to-love addition to our family. I will make the arrangements and send you the ticket. What day will you fly?"

"It seems the 4th falls on a Wednesday, and I only have that one day off. I will have to ask for some time off from my intern position with my Attorney General and the Civil Rights position with Judge John Ford. It may be too much to ask at this time in my career. I will have to get back to you. However, I will try to get Thursday and Friday off. If I can manage that, I would fly to you on Tuesday afternoon and return home on Sunday afternoon. You can arrange the times for tickets, but keep them within these days and times. Okay?"

"Okay, that sounds like a plan. I will arrange everything. I am so excited. My grandparents are going to be so thrilled. We will be cooking extra special dishes just for you."

The weeks moved at the speed of molasses dripping out of a jar, but each day was filled with exciting events in both the AG's office and the few hours Jen worked for Judge Ford on matters of civil rights. She was so enthralled with the work she was doing in the law that life went on joyfully for her. Jen's father and Robert's father had created a business partnership and were looking at land further north in Middleton. They decided to build a shopping center strip on one side of the property and on the other side a professional office building for doctors and attorneys. Her dad had suggested that Jen take one of the offices and Bobbie take another. Well, it all sounded perfect for her dad, but Jen began to feel strapped—trapped—and that feeling she never wanted to feel. She never liked feeling trapped. She felt that the few days spent with Brason's family during the 4th of July would better help her to determine just what her life with him would be like. It would be a revelation upon which she would be able to make a judgment based on facts without all the mixed emotions she had built up. It would have been easy to relax and take each day as it unfolded before Robert's passionate kiss, but now? Jen began to see her life in two segments: one as the Jen of the family she had always cherished and the other, a confused Jen, as an addition to the Brason family. It was for her to weigh the balance and observe the conditions, just as an attorney would do—facts versus emotions. She could hear her dad: "Lead with your head and a dash of emotion; otherwise, you stand the danger of making a big mistake."

The thought of seeing Brason on the 4th brought flushes of heat through Jen's body, only to be splashed with the realization that she had promised to give Robert an answer to the invitation to be his date for the formal dinner at the club on the Saturday after the 4th. It had fully slipped her mind when she told Brason she would go to his family reunion. It surely would hurt Robert's feelings, but they were long-time good friends. He would understand.

CHAPTER 25

Robert did not understand, nor did he accept the fact that Jen would spend the 4th of July with the Brason family. In fact, he was upset and embarrassed that the kiss had ever happened. How would his family take to Jen going off with a Black man and giving up the dreams they had for Robert Jr. and Jen? All of this settled on Jen's mind, and she began to think of how she would feel if everyone in her family and some of her friends turned their backs on her. How would she feel about the challenges of life without them? How would she feel without the strong support of her best friend—Robert? She now had to add these facts to the equation.

Jen felt miserable, but she still had to continue with all her work.

At the moment, she would have to submit a request for time off and hope that she would get a positive answer. If she did not get the time off, then her parents would see the tension between her and Robert on the boat trip. They would begin to ask questions. Oh, my, what a dilemma.

Several days after she submitted her time off request, Jen's papers were returned with the dates approved for her. She could call Brason and tell him that she could travel on Tuesday afternoon and be at the Brasons' until Sunday. Jen was very excited. In her eagerness to see Brason and meet his family, she allowed the thoughts of her family and Robert to slide back into her mind. This made room for her many rushing thoughts of what might happen in the July 4th meeting with Brason's grandparents and the rest of his family.

Her energy raced from what to wear to what to bring to the hostess—shorts, slacks, dresses, flowers, candy. What other things must she be ready for? Would they expect her to go to church on Sunday with the family? Should she wear a hat? A proper dress should be packed. Oh, yes… a sense of humor, too. That is probably what most definitely MUST be packed. The real excitement came when she finally was able to contact Brason one day during the week to give the good news that she had the days she needed off.

"Fantastic, my love. You wait and see; everything will be PERFECT just as everything else we have experienced so far."

"Yes, my love. You have such positive expectations of the world. Please keep up the energy so I can feel it too. That's not always the way I feel on this end."

"Oh, Jen, don't tell me you haven't begun the dialogue with your parents?"

"Well, I have had some talks with Nonno, but he doesn't seem to think that my father will be at all agreeable to the situation, and my mother will have very little to say to support me if Dad doesn't agree. I am a little concerned."

"I will help you in any way I am able when we can spend some time together. You will see how loving my family is, and you will feel quite at home in my world."

"I'm unfamiliar with the love I have for you, Brason. I have never felt this feeling. I am really trying to understand all the elements of a racial marriage. I am researching the various difficulties that you will face in your climb to be governor and how they will affect your success. Then I must think of the challenges I will face in my career with the burden of having to help our children struggle for success through the discrimination that will be set before us."

"Listen, Jen, it will all correct itself as it should. Have faith in our love and don't be so frightened. I'm here for you. I must go now, but I will call you when I am able. Until then—I love you and eagerly wait to hold you tightly so you can feel my strength."

"Yes, Brason, I know I have missed your holding me and that you will give me the strength I so desperately need. I love you so very much, my darling. Goodbye for now."

"Goodbye, Jen, love you."

The days passed with the usual stress of going to classes, studying for exams, working at the AG's office, and putting time into work with Judge Ford. Additionally, she visited her mom and dad and tried to be happy about her visit to see Brason's family, trying not to let out to her parents that her new love interest was Black. All she would say was that he was wonderful and that they had a fantastic time together, and that he was an Attorney General, and that he was running for governor of his state. However, she had never and would never tell them what state because she didn't want that information out in the public. Her mom would tell her auntie, auntie would tell her sister-in-law, and then everyone would be talking. This way, whatever happened, it would be a surprise to everyone concerned. They would already know the excitement and the happiness that this relationship was creating in her life, and, should it fall apart, they would move quickly on to whatever else was gossip in their lives. It always happened that way. It was the best way for everyone.

The Friday before the 4th of July, Brason called early in the morning with instructions to go to American Airlines and pick up the tickets. Jen hurriedly dressed and got to work early, even though the American Airlines office opened at 9 a.m. Jen got to the office about 8:00 a.m., did her usual walk through the Hall of Flags and down the main stairway of the State House to her desk. It was a super part of her day. She prepared everything for the day, sorting files in order of priority and dates. Not much would happen on Monday or Tuesday, with the 4th on Wednesday, but the court was still in session. The law was always working. Around 10:00 a.m., Jen went out to American Airlines to pick up the tickets. She was excited, and Nancy was over her shoulder, as excited as if she were with Jen on this significant trip. She was a very sweet friend and always available to Jen. Nancy covered for Jen in the office whenever necessary. She was a true friend.

Judge Ford was taking the entire next week off, and Jen's position at the state house would be covered by Nancy. If anything drastic occurred, she would get in touch with Jen. Jen felt ready for this meeting with the Washingtons and the hope that this might resolve many issues she could not even imagine.

The weekend was filled with studying and sorting clothing that needed ironing or some that needed washing. Arranging for a long weekend trip was not so easy, especially when one had no idea of the expectations.

(Phone rings)

"Yes, Mom, I will be just fine. I have my tickets, and Brason will pick me up at the airport, and we will drive about an hour to his family farm. Yes, I have proper clothes and money in my pocket. I will be just fine. Yes, I will have a good time. Yes, I will call you when I am able to tell you that I have arrived safely. Please don't worry. I will be all right. Also, Mom, remember I am a grown woman. I know.

Okay, go out to the Island and enjoy the weekend. Talk with you soon."

They were taking the weekend and the full week for the 4th celebration. They all loved being on the water and staying nights on the Island Resort. That made her think that Robert might not be going with them for the entire time.

"I wonder what Robert is going to be doing during these days. Why would I care what Robert is doing when I'm going to meet my future husband? What is wrong with me? Why am I such a wimp? Afraid of everything! Not daring to think on my own. Maybe it's time for me just to evaluate all the bases and determine what it is that I want to do for myself. It is time for me to grow up."

Jen spent the weekend studying, doing a bit of laundry, and walking in the apple orchard in addition to playing the piano and singing. These things always placed her in a peaceful frame of mind. She enjoyed doing some of that too.

Monday came. Jen went to work as usual. On Tuesday, she packed her suitcase in the car and drove to the State House. She was blessed with an inside parking spot where she could leave her Ghia. She did her work until lunch with Nancy. Then it was time for her to get a cab to the airport. She and Nancy hugged.

"Have fun and try to enjoy the entire process, Jen. Try not to judge too much, but instead enjoy all the surroundings and watch the people you will have to live with should you and Brason continue on this path."

"Nancy, I will do my best, and you are giving me very good advice."

"Love ya, Jen."

"I love you too, Nan."

Nestling into the window seat of the plane had a sobering effect on Jen. She was actually on the journey to meet Brason's family. She was relaxed and thought about what Nancy had suggested—relax, watch, but don't be too critical. She promised herself that she would look for good in all things, just as her Nonno always said. It would be a couple of hours before Brason would meet her at the airport, so she closed her eyes and thought of him, not of the potential difficulties they would have to face.

CHAPTER 26

Brason woke early on Tuesday morning to complete the many chores that his grandma had given him for the July 4th party, and, since Jen would arrive that afternoon, his job was to take five six-foot tables out of the barn, wash them down, set them up, and place tablecloths on each of them. His grandma always gave specific details on all her projects. These tables were for the exhibition and presentation of all the homemade delicacies for the family to enjoy. Of course, some of these food masterpieces took days of preparation. Everyone loved the preparation as well as the presentation, for food was one of the most important things in the life of the African American community. They had learned to move mountains with the control of food, especially in the civil rights movement. However, today and for the weekend, it was for pure joy and a family celebration.

Brason finished his chores, showered, and dressed for his luncheon presentation, which he had promised to his constituents but would have preferred preparing for Jen's arrival. The campaign was going quite well, and the momentum was carrying through from all the events set up by the managers, and he certainly did not want to disappoint.

"Okay, Granny, I've done all you asked, and now I must go to the meeting."

"Yes, my love, but remember you almost always forget time when you are campaigning. Please don't forget. You must be at the airport by 4:00 p.m. to pick up Jen. Don't be late. Cocktails are at 6:30

p.m., and dinner is at 7:30 p.m. Jen will need some time to refresh herself before all the activities begin," she reminded him as he planted a kiss on her cheek with "yes, yes, yes," and raced toward the waiting automobile.

The luncheon was a success, and his constituents approved and supported his platform. He loved campaigning and the exhilaration all the attention brought him.

A check of his watch brought the realization that he would be late to the airport. Jen would be waiting. He started for the door, but the crowd slowed his exit. Finally free, he jumped into his waiting car.

"Hal, please get me to the airport as quickly as possible without being stopped by the police."

"Will do, boss. Relax and hold onto your seat," Hal said as he accelerated the speed and headed for the airport that would be 45 minutes away with medium traffic.

"I wonder what has happened," Jen thought as she looked at her watch for the hundredth time. She was not upset, but she was concerned that he might have gotten caught up in something he couldn't get out of. That was the story of politics and campaigning. In 5 minutes, she would have been waiting for approximately an hour. She always allowed an hour, but she had no place to go. She went to a phone and called his private number, but there was no answer. She just had to be patient and wait until he showed up.

"Why couldn't he have made an effort to be here waiting for me, or at least be on time? I would have done that for him. I promised Nancy not to be too critical, but consideration is an important aspect for me."

Suddenly, a black Cadillac pulled up to the curb, and out of the backseat, Brason jumped and raced to Jen. They embraced with a kiss that expressed their passion for each other.

"I'm really sorry that I was not on time. You've been waiting a while, and I am truly sorry. I had planned to be here waiting for you, but I got caught up in a luncheon and found it difficult to get away when I needed to. Will you forgive me?"

"This time, yes, as long as you give me your full attention this weekend."

"I promise. We will have a super 4th of July celebration for everyone, and they are all waiting excitedly for your arrival. Let's go," he said as they rushed to get into the car. Hal put the luggage into the trunk.

The ride to the farm was a pleasant excursion through the city and out into the countryside of rolling hills, trees, small lakes, and waterfalls.

"What a charming landscape."

"You will love the farm. Granny is really enthusiastic about meeting you," he said as he planted a gentle kiss on her lips.

Jen was shy about kissing Brason in front of Hal. He was a complete stranger, and she was uncomfortable with that. Virtually no human being she knew had even seen her with Brason. Hal was the first person, other than those on the night of the AG's dinner, and his college roommates. That night was formal and public. This was different. This was personal and private.

Both Brason and Jen relaxed into a proper, comfortable snuggle and fell asleep from the motion of the car. Both had done a day's work already, and they still had the evening festivities to be fully present for.

When they arrived at the farm, it was about 5:00 p.m., and a great rush of people gathered as Hal pulled the car up to the circular driveway. The farmhouse was lovely with flowerbeds in full bloom and flowering trees enhancing the landscape. The group parted, and Grandma Washington, distinguished and enchanting, came forward to greet Jen.

"My darling Jen, we are so happy to have you join us for this 4th of July family celebration."

"I, too, am delighted to be here. Thank you for inviting me," Jen replied as she handed Grandma the bouquet of flowers she had purchased at the airport just for Grandma. "These are for you."

Brason's driver, Hal, took Jen's luggage out of the trunk and proceeded to take it into the house as the entire group of aunts and children followed Grandma and Brason to the house.

"Maybe Jen would like a few minutes in her room to freshen up before cocktails," Grandma suggested. "Show her to her room, Brason."

"Come on, kid, we have our orders," Brason said to Jen in a joking manner, evoking a joyful laugh from Grandma.

Once in her room with Brason, they both reached for each other and kissed with an abandoned freedom. They had not seen each other in over a month, and phone calls did not take care of the emptiness. Now, Jen's heart was filled with pure contentment that could not exist in a phone call.

"Jen, I've missed you so much. I'm so happy that you decided to come and be with us."

"I am too. It is important that we share our personal lives together if we are truly serious about living it together. Now, go away so I can do a little magic and come to the cocktail party as the adorable kid I really am."

Brason enveloped Jen in his arms, patted her backside, and said, "Go, girl. See you in a bit downstairs."

Soon, Jen had freshened up, redid her makeup, brushed her hair into a lovely, relaxed coiffure, and put on a blue wrap-around, above-the-knee dress contrasted with a gold necklace and rings to match, suitable for the party. When she entered the room, all things stopped for that moment. It always happens. Her energy was so strong and her appearance so captivating that she stopped the conversation. It happened often.

"Here she is, finally, my love. Allow me to introduce Jenni Noveletti, soon to become one of the civil rights attorneys most likely to turn the world on its head."

"Let the festivities begin," said Grandpa. "We have so much food to taste, made by loving hands. Let us say a prayer of thanks for all that we have. Thank you, Lord, for the food we are about to enjoy and for the hands that labored to prepare it. Amen."

The evening was filled with music, song, and dance by all the young people and some very fabulous voices of the adults who had been singing in the church choir since they were youngsters. Jen got a chance to sit at the piano and play some songs she loved to sing at parties, and everyone sang with her. She felt the warmth and comfort of being part of this family. Everyone seemed to be on Brason's side in approving his selection of Jen as a possible wife, but this group was only the immediate family.

"Tomorrow is July 4th, and an entirely new group of relatives and friends are scheduled to arrive for the outside lawn party with more cousins, college friends, aunts and uncles, and tons of food to taste. You should get a good night's sleep, but before I leave you to sleep alone, you must understand that until we are engaged, we cannot sleep together under the same roof with my grandparents, out of respect for them. However, we can play for a while if you are comfortable with that, and then I will go to my room.

"I have not played in a long while. I think it will be fun. Come here, you munchkin. I've missed you so much and often fell asleep holding you in my mind, possibly triggering a dream of us both being together and making love."

"I'm here for you."

They kissed and moved to the bed. Brason did not realize how much he had missed being with Jen. Jen unconditionally made love to Brason and accepted his love with the same equal pleasure. His well-sculpted Black body felt delicious against her slim, fragile white body, especially when he gently nibbled at her breasts, arousing the juices she so eagerly required for his entry into her. It seemed as if her deep entrance and his rounded fullness matched each other's needs perfectly. As he entered her body, she lifted her buttocks to allow easy submission. He took advantage of her lift and slowly, with tenderness, pressed himself deeply and fully into her. The lovers moved their bodies to fully experience the joy of each other's love. They continued with Brason fully brushing against the walls of her vagina until neither could hold the intensity of their lovemaking any longer. It propelled both of them into that heavenly bliss that depleted them to sheer exhaustion while leaving them wanting more, until the ejaculation of warm sperm flushed into her body for the night.

"My darling, I love the way I feel with you being inside me and how empty I am without you, but I do have some of you. I will sleep very soundly, even though you must sleep in your room. I understand and love you for your principles."

"I love you, and we will have all of this in our future; I promise. Now, have a good night's sleep. I will knock on your door tomorrow morning at 8:00 a.m."

Sleep came quickly for Jen while Brason, upon entering his room, continued to do some campaign work before climbing into his bed. But when he did, all the excitement of the day washed over him.

"Thank you, Lord, for all I have before me. I will try to live up to it. Amen," he said, and he slept like he hadn't slept in months.

CHAPTER 27

(A knock on Jen's bedroom door; the clock reads 8:00 a.m. Jen is putting on some lipstick and feathering her hair.)

"I'm coming," she called as she opened the door to a handsome young man standing with a cup of coffee in his hand for her. "I thought you might like this to start?"

"Have I told you today that I love you?"

"As a matter of fact, you have not," Brason joyfully remarked.

Jen reached for him and gently kissed his lips. "Well, let me tell you how much I love you." As Brason entered the room for a brief but really good kiss, he stopped.

"Okay, enough of that for now. Grandma has breakfast ready for us on the patio, and then we drive our trucks downtown to watch the greatest little parade ever. When we return home, all the tables will be set with the tasty treats that the families have cooked for this celebration. Be certain to wear a hat to protect from the hot sun."

"Okay, I have just the hat to match this outfit," she said, and off they went to breakfast.

"Good morning, Jen!" his grandma greeted her with a welcoming smile and a hug. "I hope you slept well and are ready for a really long day."

"Yes, thank you. I slept really soundly. The mattress is so comfortable. Yes, I am ready for all the thrills this day has in store."

When breakfast was finished, Jen got into the truck with his grandma and grandpa, and a few cousins who had stayed the night. Everyone was dressed in red, white, and blue celebratory fashion. Some wore cowboy boots and cowboy hats; others wore shirts and shorts, slacks, T-shirts, and other items created from flag material.

Jen watched as family trucks pulled onto the farm and children helped their parents carry the prepared food to the tables Brason had set up for them. Some of the families left their mom behind and climbed back into their trucks to create a line of trucks going to the parade. Brason had the lead truck and found a location at the top of a hill from which the family could watch the parade. It had to pass just in front of where they parked and continued on their way to the shed where the refreshments awaited those who were in the parade.

The 4th of July was a sparkling, sunny day with the U.S. flags flying throughout the farm and along the road to the town, where preparation for their annual parade was taking place. The city always had the most interesting participants in this celebration. There were children pulling their pets in wheelbarrows, people showing their vintage automobiles dressed in vintage style, a Miss Hospitality waving to the crowd while sitting on the open convertible with two members of her court, and politicians shaking hands with potential voters. There was an energetic high school band headed by Mr. Jones, and a boombox carried by the most adorable little 4th grader that gave the back end of the parade another sound as it passed the enthralled lovers of parades. This simple hometown display of love for the country and a deep respect for democracy excited everyone.

"Jen, let's go inside the shed just for a second. There are some hands I must shake. Do you mind?"

"Remember what your grandma said about not getting involved. 'Brason, don't get involved today,' your grandma warned as we were leaving. You promised her."

"We won't be long, I promise."

"Don't worry. Today will be a family day without interruption by politics. We will drive back to the house with Tyrone."

"No, Brason, I don't mind, but it seems your grandma does."

"We won't be long. I'll be home in a jiffy, Grandma."

Back at the farm, his grandma inspected the setups and had a kind word for each of the families who had done such a great job in preparing for the event. However, she was visibly upset as she kept looking at her watch, noting that Brason had not returned from the parade festivities. It was time to say grace over the food and give thanks for all that each member of the family had achieved, and Brason was not on hand yet. They could not begin without Brason. His grandma was irritated, and it showed on her face—until she saw the truck racing down the road with sand dust flaring behind the wheels and Brason driving the beast. Brason and Jen arrived and rushed to where his grandma held the microphone of the PA system.

"Please, my dear Brason, we are ready for a prayer at the tables, so would you please settle down and begin the party festivities?"

Brason took the microphone and began his prayer:

"Dear Lord, you have blessed our family and friends abundantly, for which we thank you. You have been our shield. You have made us the greatest nation on earth. On this Independence Day, we are reminded of those who have sacrificed for our freedom, following the example of your son, Jesus. We are grateful. Bless the food we are about to partake in and the loving hands that have prepared this feast. Amen. Now let's eat and party."

Suddenly, the music began, the children played tag and ran around the tables, the cooks stood beside the table of food they had prepared, and all the guests grabbed plates and utensils, reached for food to fill their plates, and searched for a table to sit with family and friends.

Brason was so proud of Jen; he joyfully moved through the crowd, introducing her to the entire family. Jen was so happy. Everyone was so kind and accepting of her. As she and Brason continued to stroll through the crowd, Jen noticed someone she thought she had seen in Boston, but with so many new faces, she could not be certain. As the afternoon light turned into the evening shadows, the lanterns cast a soft mantle over the farm and across the sparsely filled food tables. No one could complain that there was not enough delicious food. Everyone moved from the food tables to the entertainment corner, where a few guitarists were warming up for the evening concert for their grandma and grandpa's guests. Music like "I Can't Stop Loving You" (Ray Charles) and the music of Aretha Franklin, Diana Ross, Sam Cooke, and Otis Redding set the tone for the music program. Many of the young people had begun singing at a young age in church and often tested themselves in performance at family gatherings and weddings. Some were really ready for the stage, but this practice stage was wonderful for families to enjoy while the performers practiced their trade.

"Jen, how about singing something for us?" Brason encouraged.

"Well, if you want to clear the party? Really, I would love to sing for your family. Does any guitarist know Aretha Franklin's 'Try a Little Tenderness'?"

A guitarist about her age came to the center of the stage and said, "I've got it in any key you wish."

"Okay, just in Aretha's key." Jen sang.

Jen ended with a bow. "Thank you, and be nice to each other."

The musical entertainment went late into the night for anyone who wished to take the mic. Brason walked Jen to her bedroom, where they sat looking out the large bay window onto acres of fields behind the barn. The party scene began to thin as the early morning sunrise crept over the horizon.

"Brason, this has been a wonderful day, and so many of your relatives have been so kind to me. However, I could see in some of the eyes that they like me, but some also have fear in them. I spoke to a very beautiful young woman, a little older than me, who sat beside me at one point. She began to tell me how difficult it would be for me to handle being your girl. She thought I was too 'Pollyanna-ish' and way too young and inexperienced. What do you think she meant?"

"Don't put anything anyone says in your mind. Just pay attention to us and what we feel for each other. Think about how we will manage to fulfill our destiny."

"Okay, but we really have a great deal to learn, or maybe only I have a lot to learn, about what we will face as a mixed-race couple. I have been so sheltered. I'm really trying."

"Just know that I love you, and we will marry after you take and pass your Bar exam. We will begin our life together. You must be very sure of the steps we will take because it will be a difficult journey, but we will be happy and successful as we move forward."

After a feverish kiss, Brason left Jen to sleep and think about the day and review her time with some of the people she would be living with in her future. As Jen prepared for bed, she could still hear some of the last partiers in the fields. She especially revisited the words of the girl named Tasha, who had spoken with her at the party. She explained that Black men considered having a white woman as a major achievement and that Jen should be aware of that aspect of the Black man. Jen did not sleep a peaceful sleep, possibly because she and Brason had not made love since that first night of her arrival. She felt left on her own to get the feel of the family by herself, but she slept from exhaustion and remembered she was supposed to call her family at one point to let them know she was safe and having fun.

"I'll do that tomorrow morning," she thought as she drifted into sleep.

The parties seemed to continue throughout the entire next couple of days. Then, on the day she was returning home, she and Brason visited his Aunt Hazel, who was not shy about expressing the problems that mixed couples experience in these troubled times. Brason left the two women to talk while he went with his uncle to look at fences. Jen and Aunt Hazel were left alone. She asked Jen how much she knew about how fathers of white women could commit their daughters to asylums when they found out they were fornicating with a Black man.

"I don't think I have heard anything about that."

"Have you spoken to your father about your decision to marry Brason?"

That question stopped Jen in her tracks, since that was the most difficult thing she had had to consider so far. Would her father do that? If he is a real conservative, he might.

"No answer, huh?" she continued. "Do you know that under the Law of Coverture, a woman's rights could be subsumed by an immediate male family member or a husband, and she could be certified by a physician for admission to an asylum for an indefinite period of time and without her consent or a public hearing? My darling little girl, I am the 'mouth' of the family, and I will always tell you the truth of the Black existence. Brason is an idealist and a dreamer, but he is a man. They have benefits women do not have. For your benefit, read the works in the National Library of Medicine by G13 grant recipient Kylie Smith, a historian, as part of a Mellon Foundation program, 'Jim Crow in the Asylum: Psychiatry and Civil Rights in the American South.'"

"No, I am ignorant of the many things, although I am more aware of the segregation and desegregation that are causing great street wars and destruction of neighborhoods."

"That is a beginning, my dear child, but it is only visible in the schools. It is disastrous when it is in the hospitals and the asylums. Do you know that Black babies have a greater death rate than white babies? I'm not certain of the date, but during the same time in the 1960s, a decision was handed down by Judge Frank M. Johnson of Alabama that ended segregation in the state's psychiatric hospitals, and many whites, though segregated, were caught in the mess. Think clearly about how you and your children will be viewed. Will they be considered white, or will their mixed color relegate them into the hatred and bigotry of the Black community?"

"Brason, I'm so glad you're back. It's getting close to the time when I will have to pack my things and get to the airport," Jen said gratefully.

"Yes, I am certain you are ready to go. Aunt Hazel can really be expressive. I hope she didn't frighten you. She is the 'mouth' of the family, but she loves us and wishes us happiness."

"I'm sure of that," Jen said with a loving smile.

Then it was back to the farm for Jen's luggage, where his grandma and grandpa said their goodbyes with hugs, kisses, and joy that Jen would come to visit again. Everyone bid Jen a safe trip home with wishes that she would come again for another wonderful stay with everyone.

CHAPTER 28

It was July—hot, humid, and raining—when Jen arrived at Logan Airport to pick up her orange Karmann Ghia for her ride back to her safe, quiet house in the country. Jen was very tired but emotionally stirred by the conversations between her and the various people at Brason's home.

As she drove on the I-95, Jen thought, *"My heavens, Aunt Hazel was really quite a lot of emotion to handle, but with some very valid issues to investigate."*

"Ratasha, the young woman who called me Pollyanna-ish. Well, I must think a bit about her remarks. She might very well know more than I could see at first. I must look closer."

By the time Jen arrived at home, she was more than exhausted; she felt a sore throat coming on. She did not feel up to calling her mom and dad, but if she didn't, her mom might send the police to be certain she's home and okay. Her mom had done this little number before, calling the police, until Jen stopped her, stating, "What will happen if I really need the police? They will say, 'Oh, that's the crazy girl that lives alone in that house and her mother checking up on her.'" Her mom stopped.

As Jen pulled into the driveway, the sun popped through the clouds for a moment, flooding over her lovely cottage and filling her heart with joy. She was very happy to be back home.

She took her luggage inside, and before anything else, she picked up the phone and first called Brason to thank him for a fabulous family holiday, but she could not reach him. She then called her mom.

"Hi, Mom, how did your weekend go?"

"I'm so glad you're home. I didn't want to call you while you were away, but Nonno is in the hospital. He suffered a setback with his heart, and the two surgeries that would have stopped the flow of fluid back into the heart have not done the complete job. Now, Nonno might need to have another procedure, but his age is against it, and we are talking to the doctors. How was your time with your new friend… what's his name… Brason?"

"Mom, we had a really nice time. His family is very much like ours. The party was filled with family and friends, music and food, a country parade on the 4th of July."

"So, when do we get to meet this ghost? Dad and I are really waiting for you to tell us what is going on between you two. Are you a couple or just acquaintances?"

"Oh, Mom, do we have to talk just now? I've just put my things down, and I have a sore throat coming on. I am going to take a hot shower, two aspirin, and settle in for a very long and good night's sleep. I will call you tomorrow."

Tomorrow came, but Jen did not call her mother before she went to work. Jen did not go to work today. Her sore throat had turned into strep throat. She needed antibiotics. She called the doctor whom she had known for years. He prescribed medication to the pharmacy for delivery to her. She then called her office and school to report that she was not feeling well enough for work today. It was the first time in a long time since Jen had become ill. Jen was seldom or never sick. Jen spent the day in bed with throat lozenges and hot tea.

During the night, Jen got even worse. The throat was so sore she could hardly swallow. Her temperature had risen to 103, and her head was aching. She had not called her mom, but somehow her mom was at the front door with her dad in the morning.

"Jen, when you didn't call me this morning, I could only imagine that you were feeling really sick. I just had to come to you."

Soon her mom and dad were helping Jen into the car for a trip to the hospital. Jen felt so sick that she did not fight but submitted to going to the hospital. After being admitted, she was diagnosed as having suffered a slight collapse, a nervous breakdown from overwork and stress. The doctor, who had known Jen since childhood, wanted her to stay in the hospital for a couple of days to get her back in balance before returning to work. She had finished all her finals at the University and was looking forward to being off during the summer so she could study for the bar exam. With the holidays coming up, there would be little time for Jen to engulf herself in studies, but everyone needed something from her, and it appeared she no longer had the indescribable ability to do it all… at least for the next few weeks. The doctor prescribed a few more days in the hospital and bed rest for the coming few weeks, with limited stress before she could be discharged.

"If that were possible." Jen thought. *"Being in the hospital for a few days will help me get back on my feet. I have a lot of reality to restore in my life. Fantasy is for children, and I am not a child anymore. I have some serious questions to ask myself when I feel better."*

However, after the three days were up, Jen was still not ready to be discharged and go to her home confinement for a few more weeks. It was summer, and school was out, and the Attorney General's office was quiet with many on vacation and a functioning skeleton staff to hold the fort, so her absence did not present much of a disruption since she was scheduled for a month off anyway. Nancy was the one most upset by Jen's condition. She missed her.

Jen's mom visited her daily at the hospital. With each day, she brought homemade chicken soup, which was the penicillin of grandmothers all over Italy. Jen was thankful for that because, although she was not yet ready to go home, the soup felt good. All she wanted to do was to sleep. Her mom tucked her in and left the soup on the tray for her to eat throughout the day.

"Jen, I'm going home now," her mom said.

"And all I want to do is sleep."

"You have been working really quite hard with work, school, studying, and this new guy in your life. I truly think that you have finally bitten off more than you can chew, but we won't talk now. Let's leave it for when you are feeling yourself again. It is summer, so life is more casual, less school, more study for the Bar, and vacation time at the State House."

"Thanks, Mom, that is just what I need… time to think. I'll see you tomorrow. I should be fine and will be feeling better tomorrow. Thank you again for understanding."

As Jen's mom left the hospital, Jen fell back into bed for a long nap.

CHAPTER 29

Brason was very busy with his campaign and didn't really notice that it had been at least 10 days since Jen had returned to Boston and that he had not heard from her. He, of course, had not called her for all the reasons of the campaign. Once he realized that they had not connected, he became very concerned. He knew that there were no flight accidents on her return flight and that nothing of the sort was reported on the news, so he called the only other person he knew who might know what was happening in Jen's life—her friend Nancy.

"Attorney General's Office, Nancy speaking. How may I help you?"

"Hello, Nancy, you may remember me from my being at the AG's Conference in May. This is Brason Washington."

"Oh, of course, I remember you, Attorney General Washington. How may I help you?"

"I know you and Jen are very close, but you may not know that she and I have become an item, and I haven't heard from her in more than ten days, and I am worried. I can't reach her, and I am not ready to call her parents yet."

"Well, Jen has suffered a nervous breakdown and is in the hospital."

There was silence for a moment on the other line, then the shocked voice of Brason asked in a quiver, "Please, may I have the name of the hospital? I know you are not supposed to give out information, but I think you know I can be trusted."

Nancy gave him all the information he wanted, and they both expressed their concern about Jen. Each felt the other's pain that Jen was not well at the moment.

When Brason got off the phone with Nancy, his grandma asked what the problem was, since his face expressed that he had received extremely bad news. When he told her that Jen was in the hospital and in serious condition, his grandma brought him a cup of tea and sat with him to talk.

"Brason, what do you plan to do? Are you going to go to Boston? Remember, if you go, you will inevitably run into her family, and you haven't yet been invited to do that."

"I cannot not go to see how she is doing. I have called the hospital, but her parents have requested that she not have any phone callers and limited visitors, with the exception of family members. But certainly they will let me see her."

"Well, my dear, you know the consequences. You must do what you must do."

"I am leaving for Boston tomorrow, and I will take on whatever it is that must be taken. I've never run from a difficult situation, and this is my life. I love this girl. I want her in my life, if that is at all possible. I can't give her up, Grandma. I must go to her."

"Go then. I will help you pack and get things ready for you. You must look at your schedules and adjust them with your staff. Go now, get ready, and have a good night's rest."

Leaving in the morning had a tension Brason had not felt any time he visited Boston. Usually, the excitement of seeing Jen was so delicious that it titillated his every follicle, but today was different. The feelings were ones of caution and fear that the meeting with Jen would result in a defeat. He had never felt such fear, but he also knew that a biracial relationship would not be easy, and this was only the beginning.

The flight was pleasant, and the weather was sunny and warm. As the plane circled Logan Airport, he could see some of the places Jen had pointed out to him. The area where her maternal grandmother and grandfather had lived and raised their four daughters and four sons. Everyone was married except the two sons, and everyone had children. That was a very large family to deal with. Soon, he would pick up his small piece of luggage and take a bus to the car rental for a car to travel to the hospital near her house in the country. Now it was late afternoon as he entered and went directly to the front desk of the hospital.

"In what room is Jenni Noveletti?"

"Ms. Noveletti is in room 3225; however, there is limited visitation on her card. You will have to go to the head nurse in that unit to receive a visitor's badge. She has no visitors at the moment. Do go up to the nurses' station."

"So far, so good," he thought, *"no one to have to see yet. Maybe I can see her before any one of her parents come."*

Brason got to the nurses' station and asked to speak to the head nurse. She approached him with distinct hesitation, as he was a Black man not often seen here. It was doubtful that he would be able to cajole her into allowing him to see Jen, but he would attempt it.

"Hello, I am Jen's really good friend, and she spent the weekend of July 4th with me and my family, and I haven't heard from her since the day she left. I only just found out that she is so seriously sick. I am devastated, and I want to see her. May I?"

"Sir, I do understand your situation and that you are worried about her; however, she is not to have any visitors other than her parents and a few friends, and your name is not on that friends' list. I cannot allow you entrance. So sorry."

"Well, I will wait in the waiting room, and maybe somehow you will allow me to visit her," he said as he settled himself in a nearby chair. "I'll just wait. Okay."

Just at that point, Mr. Noveletti came to the nurse's desk, and the head nurse took him aside and told him of the visitor sitting in the family comfort room. "Do you know this man?"

Mr. Noveletti, inconspicuously, looked into the family room and saw a Black man. "No, I don't know him. I've never seen him before. Did you get his name?"

"I think he said Mr. Brason Washington. He said he and Jen had spent July 4th with him and his family."

"Oh, my heavens. So, this is what all this is about," he said out loud. "I knew something was going on that we did not know about. Thank you, nurse. I'll take it from here. However, is there a conference room where I might have a talk with this man?"

"Of course. Follow me." The nurse walked him to the Doctors' Conference Room, opened the door, and turned on the lights. "Is there anything I can do for you?"

"Yes, please bring the young man here to this room."

(Brason enters the conference room.)

"Hello, I am Mr. Noveletti, Jenni's father. Who might you be?"

"Mr. Noveletti, it is a pleasure to finally meet you. I am the Attorney General of my State, and Jen and I met when Boston hosted the Conference for the country's AGs. She came to visit me and my family during the July 4th celebration, and I haven't heard from her since. When I didn't hear from her and I called her home with no answer, I then called her office. Nancy, at her office, told me that she was sick and in the hospital. I came as soon as I could."

"Are you a visitor friend from her office, or are you—actually, what are you, and why would you come to visit my daughter? How much of a friend are you? Do you just date? I don't know that you existed as a close friend of my Jen."

"Well, Jen and I have been dating for the past two months. She was supposed to tell you, and I thought you had some idea that we were interested in each other. I'm sorry that this is how you had to find out about our relationship."

"RELATIONSHIP? Do you mean like lovers?"

"Yes, Mr. Noveletti, I am in love with Jen, and I think she is in love with me. I want to marry her and build a life with her. I'm so sorry we had to meet like this, and I'm sorry that Jen had not discussed this with you. Obviously, this is not the time to get into it without Jen being part of our conversation, Mr. Noveletti. I will stay in Boston for a few days. With your permission, I will call Jen and speak with her about our future."

"You are correct. This is not the time to discuss what Jen feels or what she is planning. However, let me talk to you as her father… a father that probably loves her much more than you, and for a lot of different reasons, deeper than you could ever begin to feel at this moment. Please do not interrupt me while I speak, because you will have your time when I have finished."

CHAPTER 30

“**M**y dear Mr. Washington, please just listen to what I must say. I don't know anything about you. What I do know is that if my daughter has spent any time with you, you must be special: That much I know of her and you. So, I will assume you are a caring, thoughtful man with a career in law, which is Jen's most precious subject. She loves the Rule of Law. So, I can comprehend the close attraction.

"Also, what is not to love about a beautiful, intelligent, kind, and loving young woman? Jen is not only kind, but she also has empathy that often causes her emotional conflicts. I tell her she is too giving and that when she feeds the 'alligators,' they not only take what she offers, but they will snap off her fingers, taking more if she is not careful. She is so damn giving that I'm certain if you have been together, you have seen her unselfish display of love. I know my daughter well, and I have loved her with all the intensity that is possible for a father to give and still hold emotions in control so as to allow her some freedom to grow in mind and body. I must say it has been very difficult to keep her as my baby for as long as I have—far too long. I am finding it most challenging to see her innocence absorbed into the engulfing world. I know she has dated a little, but with the work schedule, the law classes, and the studies, it is not much. She does have an uncanny way of organization that allows her to commit to all she needs, and especially to what she wants. She will wear herself to the bone to accomplish a difficult task. Though she appears strong, she suffers from the inability to stand up for what she needs for herself. She is not a fighter. A strong, well-thought-out defense for herself is hard to come by. She often places herself in second position so as not to hurt someone.

"I don't know how serious you both are, but your futures together pose a serious cultural and social problem to me and my family. Some states forbid you to marry. You cannot travel through states that do not recognize your marriage vows. Your children will be forced to struggle against the bigotry of hateful mobs. I did not raise my Jen to face that kind of personal hell, even for love. Love is a strange bedfellow. It is fulfilling and joyful when two people of the same background and religion commit their lives to each other with the approval of their parents. The parents will be happy for their children's life together, to face the many challenges in their lives against the world, because their core values and cultural systems are balanced. They have a good chance of survival. But with the obvious differences to begin with, in a world of hate, bigotry, and violence that will never end, at least not in my lifetime nor yours as well, it is impossible. Even your children will suffer; not only through the 60's generation but for many more years than we can imagine.

"So, I ask you, no, I beg you, please do the most difficult thing love can demand—if you truly love Jen, set her free. Give her the love you have so she can become the Jen she will become. Give her space to find who she is. It is not fair for her to go from dependency on a strong, loving family to a life of tension, fear, and terror in a racially disturbed country.

"Under no circumstances will I approve this relationship. Understand, I will not stand by and watch. I will continue to compare her life of struggle with you to the life I have planned and built for her with my blood, sweat, and tears. So, please do not disrupt our family with this incredibly destructive situation, Mr. Washington."

"Mr. Noveletti, excuse me, but Jen is awake and asking for you," the nurse said.

"Mr. Washington, would you like to see Jen? You can, if you wish."

"Mr. Noveletti, I thank you for your offer, but I think I will wait until Jen is better to see her. I will call and speak to her about how she feels going forward when she is better. I appreciate your sharing your feelings. You are correct about loving someone so much that their life becomes more important than your own life. That's a difficult decision to face. I've never been in that situation before. I must leave before I can make a proper statement. I love Jen. I want her to be the mother of my children. I cannot make any decision now. It has been an experience, an eye-opener, and a pleasure to meet you. We shall certainly meet again. Under what conditions, I cannot say. Goodbye, Mr. Noveletti and Mrs. Noveletti," he said as he exited the conference room and headed for the exit of the hospital.

Jen's parents hugged and then walked together into Jen's room. Jen was crying and in seemingly great emotional conflict and pain.

"My love, what seems to be the trouble?" her mother asked, brushing back Jen's hair from her forehead. The love that Jen felt was so great that her tears increased and shook her tiny body. Her father came and held Jen's hand to let her know that life was fine and not to worry.

"Daddy's here. We will talk when you are feeling better and have more strength. Sleep now. Tomorrow will look different."

CHAPTER 31

The weeks went by, and Jen began to feel more herself. It was time for her to call Brason and talk with him about the past weeks. She and her family had somehow reached a point where they were no longer telling Jen what to do but were attempting to tell her what they were doing for her.

"Jen, you look so much better. I think it is time for you to come home," her dad said, approaching the request to come home with them for a while with great delicacy.

"Dad, that sounds very comforting, and maybe I will come for a week or so, but I really must get back to my life. I have some very important decisions to make, and I must have a clear mind. The doctor said that if I maintain a healthy schedule and minimize the stress in my life, he will let me go home tomorrow. I think I am ready now."

"Jen, I must tell you something that I have been keeping from you because I did not think you were ready for it. Brason came to visit you. Now, don't get upset. I spoke to him as I would any man who would want to marry you."

"Oh, Dad, I'm so sorry. I should have shared with you what was happening, but I was so very frightened that you would disown me."

"Well, of course, it did enter my mind first, followed by signing you into a sanitarium. You know how I am. It hurt me so much that you did not have the faith to speak with me. It is a very heavy circumstance to be in, and you have not had the experience to make a positive, well-thought-out decision. I hope we can manage this affair together."

"Dad, I would like that, but do you think you will be able to actually understand my side of the situation? We are usually on opposite sides of many of the issues we discuss."

"Jen, I will do my best to understand. I think it's best if we wait until we get home to set up our study visuals on the big board, or are you ready to do that now?"

"No, Dad, I'm not ready to do it now. I think I must first call Brason and talk with him about our life together and some of the unsettling events that have happened during the last few weeks. Let's wait until I'm home with you, Mom, and Nonno. Will that be okay?"

"Of course, that is where you are safe. We all love you so much. It is where you can think clearly. We all look forward to your being with us even for a little while."

"The doctor will let me go tomorrow if all my vitals are good. I am ready to go home. Dad, first, I will want to go to my house to get some things that need to be done, bills needing to be paid, and some clothes to take with me for the time I will spend with you and Mom."

"Great, I'll be here tomorrow as soon as you call me and the discharge papers are ready."

(Jen and her dad hugged and kissed; both were so much more relaxed than before the secret was uncovered, and an understanding agreement for the moment.)

CHAPTER 32

The first call that Jen made on her discharge day was to her dad. She was ready to leave the hospital; he could come get her. The second call was to Brason, but she wasn't certain where he was. She called his usual personal numbers and finally got him at his campaign office in Boston. He had decided to stay for a week in the hopes that he would have the opportunity to see Jen.

"Oh, Jen, what happened? It's so good to hear your voice. I love you, miss you."

"Yes, Brason, I was so sick when I got home from the weekend. I had such a fabulous time with your family. They are all loving, enthusiastically supportive of their children's choices. I just love how they treat each other. No one is afraid to say what is on their mind. How fantastic."

"You also must know, Jen, that your dad and I met. I came to the hospital, but at first, he would not allow me to see you. Instead, he invited me into a conference room where we had a conversation; granted, it was rather one-sided. I did not think it proper for me to be discussing us without your being in the conversation as well. When can we see each other?"

"I'm going home today. My dad is coming to get me, and he will take me to my house to do some things, pick up some clothes, and then go to their house for a week, or until I'm really back on my feet. I am so weak I will need Mom's help, especially if I am going to be studying for the Bar exam."

"OK, I will stay in Boston for the week, but then I have a tour set up that I will travel by bus across the northern portion of my state. I will be out for about a week. After that, I can return to Boston. It will be autumn, and the leaves in the orchard should be turning bright colors. A perfect time for us to spend a weekend and talk."

"Brason, that sounds 'perfect.' There's that word again, but let's keep everything on hold for a bit until my dad and I have had our discussion."

"I'm glad your dad has discussed what we talked about. I was certain he would not tell you that I was at the hospital."

"Yes, he told me just yesterday when he knew I was feeling better and the stress of my being ill was gone. No, we haven't discussed anything yet. Our plan is to keep that for the days I will be spending with them, and my health improves significantly. I really didn't realize I was stretched so thin; it was affecting my health."

"Jen, I had no idea. I have some time off. I would like to plan a weekend for us in the mountains to see the changing of the leaves and the beautiful colors of the Blue Ridge Mountains during autumn. My cousin has a log cabin in the Valle Crucis area. It's called The Cozy River Cabin. It will do us both a world of good. Plus, we will need that rest in order to be ready for what's to come. Your Bar Exam and my primary. What do you say?"

"That sounds lovely, but the weekend at my house sounds even better. I will confirm the dates when I get to my parents' house."

"Done! We will talk when you get home. Love ya so much."

"Me too! Talk later."

As Jen put down the phone, her dad entered the room with flowers for her and pastries for the nurses' station. "Everyone has been so helpful in taking care of my Jenni. Thank you all for your services," her dad said as he pleasantly greeted the staff.

Jen gathered her things; her dad helped her, and they left for her house. The ride to her house was short; conversation was shorter, but both father and daughter were happy to be together. As Jen's house came into view, her heart skipped a beat. She loved her house so much that she could never imagine giving it up, but she would have to should she and Brason decide to marry. She would have to go to his work location, and she would have to form new relationships. She had not given any of these issues any attention, but she had to, and soon, before everything got out of hand. They parked the car and walked to the front door, unlocked it, and entered the house. It had been locked up for almost three weeks and needed some of the cool air that was now beginning to come to the country.

When Jen opened the sliding door to the kitchen, the shock of what she saw produced a shrill cry.

"Oh no, what the fuck is this? What has happened? Who could have done this?"

What Jen saw was all her Christmas ornaments, Christmas tree and lights, winter clothes that she stored in the attic, and photo albums on the floor of the kitchen. The pull-down ladder to the attic was down, and as she and her dad walked through the kitchen into the guest room, they saw the bed had been pulled apart, and the wall had been written on with a magic marker. As they walked down the hall to the master bedroom, Jen saw her clothes out of the closet on the floor; mirrors had notes like "nigga luva, you bitch" written in lipstick. All this was enormous for Jen to handle. She sat down in the living room and cried—a very deep, agonizing, painful cry. Was this a sample of her future life? Her dad just sat beside her, saying nothing, thinking more thoughts than he wanted to say right then. This moment was for Jen to absorb. For her to take it all in. It was her life; she would do as she saw fit. All her dad did was hold her, assuring her that nobody or anything would hurt her with him there to protect her. She was safe. Jen felt all he was feeling. She cried until all the crying was out of her. She was already exhausted.

After a few more tears, her dad suggested, "I think we must call the police to report the break-in, then the insurance company. After that, we will clean up the house. I will stay with you tonight so that if you are being watched, they will see that you are not alone and that someone is here with you. Also, let's call Mom and ask her to come. She will be helpful in putting your things back together. However, nothing can be done until the police come and do whatever they must do. I'm going to make some tea for both of us. Also, the house is a bit chilly, so I'm going to put on a little heat to take out the chill."

Whatever her dad was doing was acceptable to Jen. She was completely absorbed in the scene that had messed up her lovely home and left behind as a statement of ignorance, bigotry, and hate. She deserved none of this, but she could see what her life would be like with Brason ever so clearly. It was real, and it hurt deeply. She cried agonizing tears.

The day was one of noting lost items that were simple treasures from Jen's maturing life. Some of her clothes had to be thrown out since they were torn and soiled; other items needed repair as they were broken from being thrown across the room. Photo albums that were torn needed to be repaired, and photos placed again into new albums.

That day, life changed for Jen. She would call Brason to tell him of her unexpected homecoming present and confirm she would be with him for the planned weekend date. After all, they had much to talk about, and she needed the time together to discuss how the future would be for both of them. She also had to test what she really wanted for her life. She was accustomed to just going on the path set out before her. Now was the time to grow up and determine the road to her future. For now, the situation at hand had to be stabilized before she could move forward.

The police came, documented the incidents of the time, and took photos of the rooms and the destruction left behind by unknown offenders.

"Anyone after you? Who might it be? Have you had arguments with anyone in the area? We will watch your property over the next couple of weeks, just in the event that they might come back again," the police questioned Jen.

After the officers left, her dad called the insurance agent, who instructed him on what documents to send and assured him he would handle the rest. Her mom arrived with soup, a smile, and her comforting words: "It will all turn out fine. Don't worry. Daddy's here. And now I'm here, my beautiful girl."

They all cried more tears, but when the crying was over, the three were still hugging together. It all seemed just another incident in the daily lives of regular people who loved their family and each other. They would face it all together.

Both her mom and dad stayed the night with Jen. Her mom had breakfast ready when Jen woke. She had slept well… no bad dreams, no headaches, just black, alpha-level, soundless sleep. The following weeks went quickly as Jen grew stronger while staying with her family. Life began to slide slowly back into the normal she understood. She continued to work with the judge but spent fewer hours at the State House. The attorney general's office was being moved out of the State House and into a modern multi-story building. Jen was not very happy about that. She loved going to the State House every day. It would not be the same. Jen continued to study with her 2 friends at Suffolk and went to lectures with them. One day, a representative from the Pentagon came to Suffolk to offer a one-year, all-expense-paid program in human rights to students in the top 1% of the class. Jen was in that group, as were Jaimie and Sasha, but only Jaimie wanted to go. Sasha had other offers and wanted to begin working as soon as she passed the bar. Jaimie wanted Jen to go with her, but because Jen was so wrapped up in a love affair with Brason, she had been uncertain. But now, it was a program to be seriously considered. She would talk with her dad, her mom, and Nonno, who was doing well with his heart problems.

After spending several healthy weeks with her family, taking such good care of her, it was time for Jen to return to her home. She had to begin living her life again. She made an outline of events for the coming months and year. She would make her list and prioritize items that were important to her. She would then list those that were important to her with Brason. She would not call Robert. It seemed he had another girl in his life, which disturbed Jen, but she didn't see it as her problem.

"Enough!"

She would think seriously about the program and taking a year off—either in Prague, at the United Nations, or somewhere else. Once she had everything outlined, she and Brason would be able to go over the issues and make decisions based on what Jen expected her life to be and how his life fit hers. For now, daily life was going along well. Robert had visited her in the hospital. He had called to see her for lunch at her mother's, but he seemed mentally occupied with other things. He was, as always, waiting to learn what she would decide for her life. He still loved her. Were it not for that accidental kiss, he would not have bothered waiting for her with Brason in the mix, but there had been something in that kiss. Was it only he who felt it, or did Jen feel something too? Jen was worth waiting for. He didn't want to go to the top of his dreams without her. However, his date on the 4th of July had turned out to be quite charming, lovable, and agreeable to his dreams. She was an architect. He had met her during one of his land-development visits to Aspen with his dad and Jen's dad. Both fathers were quite impressed with her. However, Robert was not giving up on Jen, but he was not going to be ready whenever she called, either. She didn't call him, and he hadn't called her either.

Jen placed Robert's kiss in the pile of pros and cons of her love affair. But after the break-in at her house, the cleanup, the insurance company, and the police, she had additional issues to place in the package. However, first she wanted to speak with her dad, mom, and Nonno. She planned to speak with them together over a bottle of wine and delicious specialties. Jen spent days at her parents' house, feeling the love and comfort their protection gave her, but never discussed anything. Also, all the housecleaning, clothes washing, grocery shopping, and cooking were done by her mom. What a pleasure!

"Mom, Dad, Nonno, my time staying with you has been a joy, and the rest has made me not only stronger in body but in mind. When I go home, I would like you all to come to my home for an open discussion about my future. I want us all to agree. Not necessarily to agree on each of the issues, but to agree that I will have to make the final decision, and the family will have to support what I decide, because I am a grown woman, or disagree and accept the conditions. Is that okay?"

All agreed. They chose a date.

Jen set up this gathering a few weeks after she returned to her home. She invited them to her house so she could be on her own turf. She prepared snacks of the specialty items her dad liked and the wine he enjoyed on special occasions. They all arrived together in her dad's car. They all kissed, hugged, and complimented Jen on how beautiful the landscaping was and how homey and comfortable her home looked after the total disaster. Jen arranged this meeting with all the positive enthusiasm embodied in her being. She did not want to have this turn into a yelling, argumentative, and destructive gathering, which sometimes occurred between Jen and her dad. Those discussions always ended with Jen saying, "Okay, Dad, it's time for me to say bye—bye, bye. 'Til next debate!" Jen did not want this to happen. What she wanted was acceptance of whatever decision she made, even if it was not the decision they wanted for her and even if it might not be the best decision for Jen herself.

(The family arrived. After kisses, hugs, and laughter, everyone settled into seats at the dining room table.)

"First, Mom, Dad, and Nonno, I'm so happy that you came to my home today. I want to thank you for all the attention that you have given me during my recovery. It showed your love. I love each one of you more than you can imagine. This situation was not meant to happen in this way, but since it has unfolded, and you all know that I have been seeing this fantastic Black man for the past months. He has expressed his love for me and his desire to marry me. I think I love him, but I'm not certain that I really know what love is. Yes, I have had a few boyfriends, but nothing that would be considered undying love. Robert is my friend, yet he and I have never even had a date. I like him, and I could not, and would not, want to have him out of my life. I have considered him in this puzzle, too."

"Jen, I would like to speak first, if you don't mind. I think I also speak for Mom and Nonno, but they will say something after me if they wish."

Her dad began to speak in a strong, forward tone, as though what he felt was written in stone, and there would be no flexibility in his belief—only deep anguish for a child he loved more than life itself.

"I love you, Jen, above all things in my life. I want all the wonders of life to be yours. With that in mind, as I listen to what you want, or think you want, it appears that you have not truly reviewed all the issues. We both know that I want the same things you want: love, a fine home, family, and a successful career in the law. I believe almost all that you believe in, except for your uninhibited love for the good of the world without critical study. I am not a bigot. I have nothing against people of color. We had Sicilian members of our family who were very dark brown. One of them, we used to call her 'Blackie.' Her life was not easy because of her darkness. As for slavery, every nation has had slavery at one time or another. It is a universal practice as far back as early civilizations and societies worldwide, including Africa, Asia, Europe, and the Americas. As a matter of fact, people in Sicily were enslaved most significantly during the Roman period, when the Island was a major source of slave labor for the Roman Empire, especially for its agricultural estates and mines. Sicilians fought for their freedom against their Roman masters because they faced extremely brutal conditions, long hours, mistreatment, and sometimes being shackled at night. So, you see, I am not a bigot, but a father who understands not only our past but our future.

"My father left Sicily in the late 1800s, but not before he married Grandma, who was 18, and your grandpa was 25 years older. Your grandma had 14 pregnancies, with only 2 sisters and 3 brothers surviving. It was hard… very hard. One sister died at 12 years old from a natural childhood disease since there were no vaccines. If there were, we could not afford it anyway. Life became even more difficult when my father died, leaving the family with no possibility of survival except to take me out of school to go find work. I scrounged for food, gathering whatever possible droppings from the food carts in the market to create dinner. I made a shoeshine box and went to the meat markets to shine the shoes of the workers. I found wooden boxes that fruits and vegetables came in, discarded as trash, but for me, they were precious finds for heat in the coal stove in our 4th-floor walk-up, a 3-room unit with no heat, no hot water, and no bathroom, only a toilet in the hallway closet utilized by 2 other families. At least we had a roof over our heads, and Grandpa's portion of ownership of the boat brought in a few dollars. I was too young to fish. Our life was difficult. There is pain in being poor. Poverty is painful. I have worked all my life to get us out of poverty. I know that you will never have poverty to face because you and the man you want to marry will be financially settled; however, you will not be socially at peace, nor will your children. Should you decide that"—his voice rose in hurt—"you love this man so much that you will endure the hardships that will be a part of your everyday existence, I will not be able to stop you. I will never give you my blessing because, in doing so, I will be approving of a life of danger and strife for you. I will never do that."

He took a deep breath, his voice rising as if to indicate that he was now really, really serious.

(His voice was now out of control with tears welling up into his words.)

"Jen, I can't agree to it if you choose to take this devastatingly, disastrous road. I will not be able to watch your children, my grandchildren, go through hateful experiences that may hurt their little souls. I cannot… I cannot. Jen, you will kill me! Please don't take that step. I will not be able to watch it."

He sat down and cried.

Her mom, who was sitting beside him, reached over, kissed him on the cheek, and gently patted his back, indicating both that she felt his pain and that he needed to calm himself down because this outburst would get him nowhere. She agreed with him. Nonno said nothing. He just lowered his head and quietly cried.

Jen stood quietly for a few moments. Her heart thundered, and her eyes shimmered as she attempted to stop the tears that had welled up in her eyes while her father had been speaking.

"First, I must tell each of you how important you are in my life. I cannot think or imagine a day without you in my life." She paused for a long beat to find her voice—its truth, strength, a mixture of grief, defiance, clarity, and love. Her voice was not angry, but measured, clear, and even.

"I always thought I understood you, Dad," she said softly. "You loved me and protected me. You worked hard to give me everything I needed. I am grateful for all of it—the piano lessons, the voice lessons, the day camps, all mixed with love. I do, I really do understand, but I never thought that my choices in life would be so attached to your dreams."

She got up from her seat across from him and swiveled his chair, so he faced her. She knelt before him, not backing away from the pain between them.

"But somewhere along the way, you convinced yourself that love had to come with limits or restrictions. That it could only look a certain way, travel a certain road, and fit your dreams. You gave me strength; you educated me; you gave me a stubbornness that has taken me through stressful times, and I have prevailed. You cannot ask me to ignore the hard issues I will face or to back down simply because they are difficult. I hadn't meant to fall in love. Not now. Yes, maybe after a few years working and establishing myself in my law career. It was always my wish, and that much later, I would get married and have a baby or two. Not now. But here it is, and I must make a decision that will be my life. My life, not what anyone else wants for it. It is mine, and I will do what I believe is right for me, regardless of the consequences."

Jen hugged her dad and returned to her seat, crying.

The refreshments were never touched, and her dad rose from his seat, wiping his eyes. "I think we have said all we need to say. It is your life, and you are the one who will make this decision. We will be beside you until you choose. Should you choose Brason's life, then you understand we are lost to each other. Should you choose something else, we will return to discuss our lives moving forward."

Everyone got up from their seat, hugged, and kissed as they wiped their tearful eyes. They would always love each other, but what lay ahead was unknown. Jen hugged each of them and waved as they got into her dad's car. Jen went back into the house and went to her special spot on the sofa by the window.

She was not ready to talk to Brason just yet, but she did want to see him soon. She needed to look more seriously not only at the issues that had arisen during the few months they had known each other, but also to take a closer look at the man himself.

"Who was he? How did he think about what she would have to give up for him?" They had not even spoken on these issues because he was always so busy with his career. *"What about mine? What if I don't want to have children right away? I know I am not the type that stays at home just waiting for my man to return. I am a worker. I do whatever it takes to get a job done, and that might take me to areas that would disturb family life. How would he feel about that?"*

Their being together to discuss all of this was really necessary. She would call him and invite him to come within the month.

CHAPTER 33

Jen spent the day in her office trying to reach Brason, but with no success. She knew that separation would be a part of their lives that she would find upsetting, whether he was Black, Brown, white or any color. She looked at her calendar, and the week of October 10 would be the height of color, not only in the backyard and the apple orchard but every tree in the neighborhood.

"It will be wonderful, and I will have some delicious food prepared, and we will decide together what is best for me and for him."

She tried his number again and let it ring for longer than usual. Someone picked up the phone.

"Washington for the Governor's Office, how may I help you?"

"Hi, this is Jenni Noveletti calling for Mr. Brason Washington."

"Yes, please wait one moment. He is just finishing a presentation, or I can have him call you."

Jen thought for a moment—"No, I will wait a moment. Please let him know I am on the line."

After a short wait, Brason came on the line. "Hello, my sweetheart. I've been so busy. Everything is going so well. The figures are through the ceiling. How are you? Have you chosen a date?"

"Yes, I miss you, and I am trying to grow up and know myself. I've enrolled in a program called Silva Mind Control. Our facilitator is a handsome young man called Ken."

"Do I have to worry about him?" Brason jokingly asked.

"No. Don't be silly. Ken has a girlfriend he is in love with and will marry soon. I'm learning to use more of my mind, and it is helping me ask the important questions to get to know who I really am and what I really want in this life. How to control my feelings, balancing my heart with my intellect to obtain a proper result for me. It is not easy!"

"Sounds good, but you can tell me all about it on—what is the date?"

"I think October 10 is the height of color in New England, and if you can make it, I think that would be perfect."

"Okay, gotta go. I'll put that date in my book, have reservations made, and we will talk between now and then. I really do miss ya, sweetheart."

"Yes. Me too! See you soon."

When Jen hung up, she felt a certain inner control that she had never felt before. Usually, she felt that she could not breathe after hanging up the phone with Brason. She felt so alone without him. Something had changed. She was certain that she cared for Brason, but the lust and the painful need seemed to have changed. Both became more real and controlled, though she could only guess that the experiences of the past months had brought her to this new point in evaluating this special love story. It was the first love story, but certainly not the last. There was so much life ahead. She was actually growing up.

The weeks went by, and Jen began closing down some of the activities that were no longer necessary in her life. She called the realtor for the funky studio apartment on Beacon Hill to say she would not extend her lease. She went to Human Resources at the State House and gave her date of resignation. She would keep her hours with Judge Ford, continuing with the civil rights cases that he was handling. She really liked working in the office of the Judge. At least now she could handle her life with more control and less stress. Facing Brason and the bar exam is enough for the moment. She was feeling ever so much better. Her space was more beautiful than she ever imagined, her parents were softer and kinder than ever, and Nonno only shed tears when he looked at her, saying, "You are so beautiful, and you have so many fulfilling experiences before you if you choose the path that is right for you." Life right now was very much better.

The weeks went by, and Jen had cleaned and refreshed her home. Her dad had sent a carpenter to paint and clean, and the house showed no signs of what existed on that horrible day she entered her home to find the disaster. It took time and money to put everything back together again.

"What must it be like when Black people's homes are burned down. What and how are they able to turn their life back to what it was before?" she thought. *"Yes, it costs money and hard work, and often even that is not available to them."*

It made her very sad to think about it, yet so happy she had the advantages that her dad provided.

(Jen and Nancy are at the office packing the many items that would be taken from the State House into the new building just a block away by the movers.)

"Jen, I don't think that I am going to like being in that magnificent new office building. I will miss the tradition of the offices here in the State House. But most of all, I will miss seeing you every day. No more vicarious thrills. I will just have to find my own."

"Nancy, you will be just fine. You are up for a promotion, and you have a great job working with the best attorneys for the benefit of the people, and as a civil servant, you have job safety, retirement, health, and all the excitement politics and the politicians can bring. And don't forget the boiler room parties." At that, Nancy threw a large paper clip at Jen.

"Don't you dare," Jen warned, as she dodged the clip Nancy threw at her.

"I don't go to the political parties. I go to kids' parties. But I do worry about some of the upcoming politicians in the game. I understand that they have cookout parties for the 'Boiler Room Girls,' who work on campaigns. They all love to party, but the girls who go to those parties are usually single and in their early 20s. The politicians rent houses for the weekends on tiny islands accessible only by ferry from Edgartown on Martha's Vineyard, like Chappaquiddick Island. There's lots of food and plenty of liquor. Too dangerous for me, plus I'm married. Too far away; just too much of everything. Oh, Jen, I am going to miss you."

"Nancy, I'm not going anywhere yet. There is still my graduation party, and who knows what else. Right now, I am trying to pull myself together so I can make an intelligent and meaningful outline of my life. I have never been in love, and this relationship with Brason has me so flustered that I have not been able to think of anything but how we have such a fabulous time alone together. Nothing else seems to matter when we are in our bubble. The one thing that I have realized is that the bubble does not follow me through the days. It only happens when Brason is at home with me. That is not a very healthy place to spend my life. I perceive myself as strong-willed and capable. I know I am many things, but this kind of love seems not to be one of them—that is, having to live a life of fear for myself, my husband, and my future children. It was terrifying to see police cars at my house and to walk in on a house messed by vandals, leaving a sense of hate in their hearts behind for me to remember."

"Yes, those were terrible moments in the past few months, but you are now well rested and can face your challenges a little easier and with greater foresight."

"Brason is coming for the weekend on October 10, which is the height of the Color in New England, and it will be a beautiful time. We will pick apples, drink cider, and make an apple pie together. We will have fun, but we will decide how our lives will go from here. My parents have been wonderful, greater than I had anticipated. They will support whatever I do; however, they will not accept a marriage between me and Brason. They are forcing me to choose, and I must be careful not to choose just to show my strength. I must show I have matured and understand all the ramifications. My choice will be based on my concept of what I want for my life. Since I don't quite know what that is, my decision is very difficult. I plan to sleep on it and decide."

"Heavens, look at all the stuff we are packing. Some of it should go to trash, but I guess we will pack it until someone tells us where it should go," Nancy said, rather tired.

"Let's just mark its contents on the outside of the box, and then they will have to decide. It doesn't really matter to me. As a matter of fact, I'm about ready to leave for the day. I have a meeting at school with the representative who came from the Pentagon with many alternatives to doing work for a year in a foreign country, to determine whether anyone is interested in working for the government. I've got lots of things to help me decide. I'll call you tomorrow."

They hugged, and Jen left for the meeting at Suffolk University. She was eager to hear about the possibility of a year in Prague. She hadn't even told her family about this possible change.

CHAPTER 34

The weeks went by, and October came with its usual beauty of colors blanketing all of Jen's backyard. She loved this time of year because the days were warm and conducive for her to put the convertible top down and drive the miles that separated her business life from her country safety. She had heard from Brason. He would rent a car at Logan so as not to have Jen hassle with the traffic and just have her be waiting at home for him as if they were married. That comment didn't sit very well with Jen. She never saw herself "waiting at home" for anyone. She had so many things she wanted to be involved in.

Jen put some Debussy on the turntable and sat in her seat by the large window, looking out at her colorfully landscaped yard. Dad had sent some lovely baskets of blooming hydrangea with the pink and purple color combination, along with the bee and butterfly area of the garden she called the Pollinator Paradise, which brought hundreds of butterflies and bees. Jen loved her home, and she had everything ready for Brason so that she could spend every minute with him. She looked at her watch. Like clockwork, it was 10:30 a.m. As she looked at some of the notes she put together for discussion, Brason pulled into her driveway. She ran to the door, opened it, and ran to him. They kissed that special I-love-you kiss, which felt so good it blotted out all other thoughts of what life had in store for them as a couple. All they understood at this very moment was that they were together after a very long separation.

"It's been so long; I've missed you so much," Brason whispered in her ear.

"I, too, have missed you so much I have no words to express how much. Take your bags inside, and I can make some coffee or tea."

"How about some champagne?"

"Let's hold that until this evening," Jen suggested.

"Yes. But I brought 2 bottles, one for our welcome back to each other and the other for serious conversation and results."

"Okay, it sounds good, just like you. Let me carry something," she said as she picked up a small package.

Once inside, Jen showed him into the guest room, just as she had done on the very first night he stayed. She told him what the house looked like when she arrived home from the hospital and the mess that had to be cleaned up.

"Brason, you would not believe how upsetting it was to see my pretty house all vandalized. The hatred hung in the air, and my heart was very sad and frightened. What if I were in the house when they decided to do it? Would they have hurt me? But let's not talk about those things right now. Let's just sit and open the bottle of champagne, put a log on the fire and continue with more Debussy."

"My sweet, I can only imagine your fear. Yes, let's put all the real world aside for the moment and let us just relive and enjoy the wonderful times we have had together. And let's plan our future."

Once Brason opened the bottle of champagne, Jen took a lovely platter of nibbles out of the fridge and placed it on the coffee table in front of the picture-window sofa.

"Jen, I wish this bubble that you speak of would float us away into Never-Never Land, away from all the evil, hatred, and unleashed anger that has filled the world."

"It is as if the 'melting pot of America,' which was what the United States was called in my dad's time, and we were proud to be Americans, holding to our language and culture at home and yet sharing with our friends the parties, dances, music, and joy of our culture. However, that understanding of our country has changed into a pressure cooker filled with those bigots embarrassed to voice their feelings in public for fear of sounding ignorant. But that premise stopped when politicians began to publicly shout from the stage words that incited the quiet, ignorant masses to finally find their voice. Those voices exploded out of the cauldron with hatred from their souls. These words of anger and hate were now allowed to escape out of their mouths because the dialogue of their leaders had become so damning and crude that it seemed okay to speak out with hurtful statements. It freed the bigots and the haters. No one was shy about saying things that would never be said among the educated in social settings," Jen finished.

"If our leaders don't control their rhetoric, the masses will just follow like puppets. That approach could lead to terrible circumstances in our country, which is why I am running for Governor. I want to make a difference," Brason added.

"That's one of the reasons I love you so much, with, of course, many other responsible and constitutional patriotic reasons," Jen said as she settled onto the sofa next to Brason, lifting her glass of champagne to offer a toast.

"Yes, of course. What shall we toast to first?" Brason questioned.

"How about the fact that we have managed to have no arguments since we met?" Jen offered.

"Okay," as Brason held his glass to hers, tapped it, took a sip, then moved closer to kiss Jen, he said, "A toast to the fact that I have thought about you every day since the first day we met," and kissed her on the lips.

"I'll drink to that," Jen said as she accepted his kiss. "Fill my glass again," she added as she intensified the kiss.

As the two kept toasting to the wonderful experiences they had had since they met, the champagne began to work its subtle magic on them. They continued the kiss into a more sensual moment. The passion in the music of Debussy and the French wine snuck up on them, and they followed their instincts, which had given way to what they really wanted at this moment. They made their way to the newly painted, suitably designed bedroom with a new bedspread and an organized closet. As the lovers closed out the world, they entered into their bubble of love. The Black velvet body of Brason entwined with the white silk skin of Jen, melted together as one tumultuous pleasure of love, joy, and sexuality.

Brason luxuriated in the softness of Jen's skin and the firm muscular strength of her body. He loved seeing her white, smooth, satin-like body draped over his muscular, Black, like velvet, buff body. He loved the feel of her firm buttocks as he felt their roundness and nibbled on the natural firmness of her breasts.

"I love you, Jen, more than you will know. I want you to be my wife. I cannot even imagine my life without you."

"I love you too," Jen said with all the true meaning of her heart.

They made love with feelings so deep that neither of them could imagine, at this moment, being without the other in their life.

Complete and satisfied, they lay in each other's arms as their lovemaking had filled them with such joy. Brason was the first to move, stating, "Jen, let's go have lunch at the little hole-in-the-wall restaurant where we lunched the last time. Let's see if the squirrel we named Squiggy is still there doing his acrobatics and stealing food from the birds."

"Sounds good to me. Then maybe we could go to the apple orchard, pick apples, and come home to make our apple pies."

"Okay, it sounds like fun," Brason responded.

"Who will be first into the shower?" Jen asked as she jumped out of bed and headed for the shower, into which Brason immediately followed.

Jen turned on the shower only to find Brason's arms clutching her, with both hands caressing her breasts; his desire still wanting more as he moved into her.

"Showering has never been quite the same since you," she whispered in his ear.

"I'm glad," said Brason, as they reached their climax, showered, and prepared to go to lunch.

CHAPTER 35

The drive through the small town, with all the colors of the autumn landscape in full bloom, felt so satisfying to Jen. She was happy that she was secure in the moment, but upon entering the little hole-in-the-wall restaurant, she felt a distinct difference from the last time. It seemed that the tone had become different, or maybe she just didn't notice it the last time. It was a definite moment.

"Let's take that table by the window," Jen said, approaching the window table, as the waitress came hurriedly to stand in front of the table by the window.

"I'm sorry, you can't have that table, it is reserved for a committee luncheon. You may sit anywhere you wish."

It seemed strange to Jen, but maybe she was just being paranoid these days; leaving the hospital and the cumulative events of the past months had left her feeling as if she were being watched constantly. As a result, Jen suggested that they go to another, more-frequented restaurant where attitudes might be different.

"I'm really not very hungry," Brason stated. "So, let's just go pick some apples and then go home, play house, and bake our apple pies. My grandma will be so pleased."

"Great. Let's drive up to New Hampshire, find an apple orchard, pick the apples, and come back home where we're safe."

It was a wonderful day of picking apples. The weather was warm from the retreating summer sun and the incoming cool October breeze, chilling the air for the Indian Summer, which produces the variety of colors of the leaves. They finished picking, arrived home, and began the preparation for baking their apple pies. Together they laughed and giggled with joy, spending the afternoon in the kitchen. While the pies were cooking, the two lovers cleared all the items used to bake the pies. Once the kitchen was cleared and back to Jen's order of perfect, the pies were ready and taken from the oven to cool. Together they went to Jen's favorite place in the living room to sit. It was time for them to do some serious talking about their lives.

The day had grown short; it was dark early. Jen sat opposite Brason in her favorite spot, looking out the picture window to the garden. Her smooth skin and wide eyes showed signs of the weeks she had spent in the hospital and the months of attempting to unravel the weight of EVERYTHING—her dad and the family's disapproval of her choice of lover, the impossible demands of her jobs, and the disaster of her loving a man—a Black man—so extraordinarily intelligent, handsome, and kind, yet she was taught never to love.

Brason spoke first as he leaned forward, looking deep into Jen's eyes, "You've been through hell, Jen. I can see it in your beautiful brown eyes. You've been carrying so much weight, more than even I could have imagined. As I take time to understand you, I am in awe of you. I am sorry if I have placed such a burden on your lovely but small shoulders."

Jen cut him off immediately, her voice weak with raw emotion.

"No, no, no! Don't you dare blame yourself. There is no blame here, only love. It is not you, my love. It is the world, my family, my friends, the politics. I see it in every glance in the street—like a verdict," she said, as she wiped the tears beginning to swell in her eyes.

"I love you, I love my parents, even when they would rather see me safe and quietly accepting their truth rather than my being truly alive with my own truth, facing my own challenges. I love the law and the lives I hope to make better from it. The thought of losing my parents is equal to their death. I can't bear the thought. Yet with you, I found a part of me that I never realized existed in me. I found a strength in your love that helped me see the depth of my love for those things I've spent my short life giving breath to. I don't know how to manage these truths without completely shattering myself." (Jen is crying.)

"My sweet, precious girl, you don't have to make any decisions right now. There is no pressure except for that which you place on yourself. Please don't do this to yourself."

"Well, there are decisions I must make soon—graduation, the bar exam in February, the Beacon Hill studio, and my country house. When I pass the bar, I have been offered a one-year place in an exchange program with the opportunity for a Master's of Law at the University in Prague, and Oxford for my doctorate," she whispered, as her eyes flickered between despair and hope.

"Oh, my love."

"If I go, it won't be to run away from you, but hopefully to find the strength to come back to you. To love you the way you deserve to be loved, in the way I want to love you—with every fiber of my existence, without falling apart. If I stay, I'm afraid I won't survive. Not like this; not now," she confessed, as tears flowed down her face, "Loving you doesn't terrify me; losing myself does."

Brason cupped Jen's tiny hands into his and lifted them to his lips for a gentle, loving kiss. He could see how very fragile she had become over the past months since he had seen her. He had not seen how close to breaking she was. It was no longer just about what he wanted or what she wanted; it was about what was a true love solution for EVERYTHING. Brason drew a slow breath to steady his voice.

"Jen, do you know what your father said to me the first time we met? He told me he raised you for a life of safety, comfort, and promise; of doors opening at every turn. He did not raise you for a life that would bring hardship, whispers, and danger around every corner. When he said that, Jen, I wanted to argue with him. I wanted to use everything I learned about proving my point. I wanted to prove him wrong, but I was silent. Tonight, I look at you, and I hear his words differently."

Jen's tears continued as Brason held her hands more tightly but gently so she could not pull away.

Brason continued, "I love you. Heaven knows I love you with every inch of my being. You are the first woman who ever looked at me and saw not the color of my skin, not my stature in the community, or the obstacles in my life. You saw just me—the orphan who is loving, caring, and ready to give his all to the woman he loves—the man. I am thankful for that."

He pressed on, though his throat thickened and the emotion he tried to hide began to show through.

"I'm talking about real love. I have that for you because real love is not about what WE want, but it's about asking what that love will do to the one we love. Will it break you? Will it steal the light from your eyes? If I keep you here with me now to fight this fight when you are not ready, what would the result be? What kind of man would make me?"

The questions created thoughts that silenced them both for a bit, with the pain of unspoken, unresolved issues.

"Maybe your father was right about one thing. Sometimes, if you love someone so much, the most unselfish act is to let them go."

As he said those words, Jen cried so deeply that her entire body shook with pain, and Brason brought her closer to himself with great love, tenderness, and understanding.

"It will be a chance for you to find your way, to experience who you are alone and what you wish from this often-ugly world. A way to find the joy in life that belongs to you. I would never steal your experiences. I wouldn't want to."

They both shed tears of love. Brason wiped Jen's eyes as he pushed back the hair that had fallen on her tear-stained face.

"I will never stop loving you, Jen, whether you are here, in Boston, or across the ocean in Prague. Whether your family embraces you or turns their back on you, you will always be in me, as certain as my breath. You see, I love you more than I can put into words. I would rather lose you to the world than see you lose yourself to me."

Jen sat very still as Brason wiped her eyes and tear-stained face. For a moment, neither one could speak. Jen was stunned by the raw intensity of what Brason had just said.

"Brason, I love you even more at this moment," her voice breaking. "Do you know what you have done? You've lifted the heaviest ache from my chest. I somehow thought that love meant choosing sides between you and my family—between my heart and my duty. It's not that at all," she said as she grabbed his hand in hers, looking deep into his eyes. "You love me enough to let me go, and somehow that makes me love you even more. Don't you see? You are not trapping me; you're freeing me. You're showing me what true love really is."

Her lips quivered as sad tears turned to happy tears. Her eyes grew brighter with joy, reflecting the overwhelming love the two held for each other at this moment.

They spent the evening listening to music, discussing what had been going on while they were separated. They talked about what the future held for both of them. Jen spoke freely about her desire to go to Prague for her Master's degree and then to Oxford for her doctorate. Jen's interest had expanded to specializing in international law, human rights, and public and criminal international law. She spoke with such joy and happiness. Brason only watched her excitement. When it was time for them to get some sleep, they shared the bathroom with each other and climbed into bed. They hugged and kissed goodnight. They would be together forever.

The morning came with the same sound of the birds singing in the trees outside. Brason got up early to pack and ready himself for his return home. Jen had breakfast going; coffee on, scrambled eggs, and English muffins ready for the plate.

There was a sadness between the two, but a glowing love that shone like the Hope Diamond, all crystal clear and bursting with potential. They had found each other in a crazy, mixed-up world. They had survived with friendship, respect, and love for each other forever. They would certainly cross paths and be in each other's lives, no matter how distant.

"That was a delicious breakfast, my love," Brason complimented.

"It will be here for you whenever you wish, only you will have to come to my mom's house. I think I will be selling my beautiful house. I will be away, and I will need the money to pay my way to Prague and tuition at Oxford. My parents will help, of course, but it really is my responsibility.”

“I will remember that. I will call you whenever I can. I love you. I don’t want to leave. It is hurting so much.”

“Yes, me too. So, just kiss me for the last time today, and let’s think about the next time.”

They kissed. Jen cried lightly. Brason picked up his bag and the nicely packaged apple pie that they had baked for his grandmother.

“She is going to love this pie, but she will be very sad for us, though happy it has been resolved with such grace and love.”

“Go before I won’t be able to let you go.”

They kissed a sweet, short peck on both cheeks as the Europeans do.

“Goodbye, Jen. I love you.”

“I love you too, Brason.”

Jen spent the day lying in bed, crying.

CHAPTER 36

(Four months later, March 1966)

Jen is buzzing around the Yacht Club, making certain that everything she had arranged for her graduation celebration and her bon voyage party is being supervised by Sharon's Party Planning. Jen checked out the guest list to be certain that everyone who had received an invitation responded positively. Was there anyone who was not coming?

Her mom, dad, Nonno, and, of course, Mr. & Mrs. Salerno were coming, as were Robert and 50 other guests, including Mr. Brason Washington. Jen was happier than her parents had ever seen her. They, too, were happy with the decision that she had made to continue with her education. Whatever would happen next was anyone's guess.

The Club was decorated with hundreds of flower baskets. It was like a fairy's garden of colors and senses. Jen looked absolutely radiant in a one-shoulder light blue, soft-fabric gown. Her hair was tied in a lovely arrangement of curls and loops. She was dazzling in her appearance. The family was excited with the arrangements, and her dad's table was set by the dance floor because, of course, there would be some dancing, as is customary at every party.

Robert came with the architect who was hired to build the ski resort that he had been dreaming of for so long. Also, Brason came with his bodyguards, but with no date.

Everyone had a magnificent time, and Jen enjoyed the party with such a free and loving heart toward everyone.

In the 18 years that passed, many events took place in Jen's life. She graduated from the course in Prague and spent a semester at Oxford, only to return to her hometown. Robert had visited her several times in Europe. She realized that she did love him. They married, had two children, and years later, Robert had almost completed the final construction of the cottages on the mountain for in-out skiing, when the heavy equipment created an avalanche, killing Robert and Jen's dad. It was a tragedy that disrupted the joy of both families and made all the newspapers and TV reports.

Jen was devastated and found life very difficult. She also believed that from bad things often come good ones. Life had been good to her, and she had many friends throughout the years. Whether in the business of law or just neighbors and friends, and especially family, she kept in touch with as many and as often as possible. Through the years, she often heard from or called her friend Brason for advice on various legal issues. Their lives were filled with the many things they loved and respectfully shared through the years. When Brason read of the tragedy in all the newspapers, he thought of calling Jen immediately, but decided to wait. When he did call Jen—

Jen is seen in her executive office in the building her dad had built for her and Robert, which she and her mom now own and operate. The enormous wealth of the family produced so much work.

"Mrs. S, there is a phone call for you. He says his name is Mr. Washington."

"I'll take it in my office," Jen said as she went to her office and settled into her comfortable chair.

"Well, hello, Brason. It's so good to hear from you."

"I hope it is not too soon or too late to call to express my sincere, heartfelt sorrow for your losses. I sent flowers but waited for a while to actually call you."

"No, it's perfect. It's been such a dreadful experience, but the children have been doing really well and understanding more about life than I could have taught them. They are fantastic. My mom has been a dream, caring for the children when I have had to contend with the volume of work our businesses produce and…"

The two best friends for life talked, and talked, and talked, and talked, and talked… (fade out)

PLAZA HOTEL, NEW YORK CITY

Christmas Season, 1985

"Ms. Jenni, here is the schedule for the day. You will meet the Senator in what was the Oak Room for a light lunch."

The ride down from the Penthouse was quiet as Jenni continued to hold onto Ian's arm. However, as they approached The Palm Court, there were photographers and people excitedly chanting outside, "Senator! Senator! Senator!" Security police were there keeping things orderly. Jen felt like she was in a movie—an old movie, but who would want her in one?

As she entered the elegant dining room, Jen thanked Ian and looked to the table where the most handsome, suave gentleman stood. As Jen approached, he held out his hand for her to take. He took her hand and kissed it, followed by a kiss on each cheek. He always made her feel like a precious jewel. The table was intimate, surrounded by lovely palms providing hiding space for the special security. The two lovers sat down to a glass of champagne and began to reflect on their lives and how Brason always kept sight of what she was doing, occasionally telephoning Jen at her office or working on a case together. Whatever happened, it was because it was what was meant to be. They just looked at each other with joy and love in their hearts, fully amazed that they were here together, finally.

"Darling, you look deliciously handsome. I've missed *us*. Your calls and legal assistance helped me through the years and have kept me working for civil rights and international rights, believing I was making a difference. I've processed so many pro bono cases for the underserved voters. Thank you."

"I have always loved you. Life wasn't ready for us."

"Nor was I." Jen smiled softly.

After lunch, they would return to the suite with a balcony overlooking Central Park for their wedding reception. Guests were expected to arrive by 5 p.m. for the candlelight ceremony. It would be extraordinary.

"It should have happened years ago, but sometimes life is not ready for the plans of ordinary people."

"Fine, I just can't believe that this is real. All the changes in my family with the deaths of my dad and my husband, Robert, in the tragic avalanche accident… I thought I could never come out of it or love again. Brason, you have always been a dream to me. It was not until President Lyndon Johnson signed the Voting Rights Act, followed by the Civil Rights Act, that I was ready to be braver and move forcibly ahead to get some teeth into my work for what I believed."

"I guess I wasn't ready for us then either!"

"Nor was I ready to be brave about what I believed. I worked really hard to use the law to make things as right as I could," Jen admitted.

"Here we are at the Plaza in what was long ago the Oak Room. It is gone, but we are still here, and I am keeping my promise," Brason stated.

"What a blessing," Jen interjected.

"We still have a lot of work to do for democracy, but we're in it together now."

Suddenly, out of thin air came Ian.

"Senator and Ms. Jenni, it is time for both of you to get ready for the ceremony, so we must go now."

(Brason and Jen follow Ian as they take the elevator to the penthouse suites, and Brason gives Jen a kiss as he leaves her off and goes to his suite.)

(The next scene at 5:30 p.m., same day.)

Jen's son, Robby, and daughter, Juliana, take their positions. At the flowered arch, Father Potter stands waiting, and music plays. Robby stands next to his sister, waiting for their mom to appear. Juliana will walk down the short aisle just in front of her mom, and Robby will walk beside his mom to give her away to Brason, who stands with Thatcher at the wedding arch. Happiness and joy filled the room as Jen's mom, aunts, uncles, cousins, and special friends took their seats together with Brason's family and friends. The music heralded the beginning of a new life together for a ready-made family of the future.

-0-

ACKNOWLEDGEMENT

I must always thank those teachers who said, "Her head is in the clouds when she writes," and those who agreed, "She has a lot to say." Both are true, and I love to spend my days writing.

To my artist-musician husband, Marlon, who never complains: thank you for all the help you give me whenever I need it. When I am in writing mode on a new book or an article, I am intense. However, he overlooks those days and waits for the sunny me to come forth. He is always a help when it comes to my computer skills. Thank you, darling, for all the assistance and for your unending emotional support.

To Hemingway Publishers, Glenn and Simon, Sarah, and all departments, thank you for guiding me through the elements from words to book publication. They have been my strength through the initial stages of the publication and onward toward marketing. I am forever thankful for your honesty, encouragement, and successful production.

To Jason Cook, the Technical Advisor at John Knox Village, for his patience, warm friendship, knowledge of computers and his teaching skills. Luv ya, Jason.

To my readers, Rae Lynch, Carolyn Morris, Sonya Perdomo, and Carolyn Van Ness, to whom I gave the first ten chapters only. "I read the 10 chapters and want more, so I began to reread the chapters again," Rae said. Carolyn said, "Excellent! I want the other chapters now." Carolyn had many suggestions, some of which I've used. Thanks to each of you for your remarks.